Disney's TOY STORY

Adapted from the film by
Cathy East Dubowski

Hippo

Scholastic Children's Books,
Commonwealth House, 1 – 19 New Oxford Street, London WC1A 1NU
A division of Scholastic Limited
London – New York – Toronto – Sydney – Auckland

First published by Disney Press 1995
This edition published by Scholastic Limited 1996

ISBN 0 590 13628 3

Typeset in Plantin by Contour Typesetters, Southall, London
Printed by Cox & Wyman Ltd, Reading, Berkshire

10 9 8 7 6 5 4 3

CHAPTER 1

It was high noon in Dry Gulch.

A few stray tumbleweeds skittered across the dusty street.

The whole town seemed to hold its breath, waiting. . . .

Spurs jangled as a lone dark-haired lawman stepped fearlessly into the street.

Jang-jangle. Jang-jangle.

Flinty-eyed, he paused, all senses alert, gun hand held out to the side. He was ready—at the twitch of an eyelid—to draw on the no-good outlaw who dared stink up Dry Gulch with his mangy hide!

The gold star on the lawman's chest glinted in the blazing noonday sun.

A shiny white plastic ring dangled from a string in his back.

At the other end of the street stood the outlaw—Mr Potato Head—with a goofy grin on his face.

Six-year-old Andy Davis reached down from the

1

sky and grabbed the dark-haired sheriff. With his other hand he yanked on the plastic ring, pulling the string.

A small voice box inside the cowboy's plastic chest squawked a scratchy pre-recorded message:

"*Reach for the sky!*"

Andy pulled the string again.

"*This town ain't big enough for the two of us!*" said the cowboy doll.

Andy shoved aside one of the moving boxes he'd decorated with crayons to create his make-believe western town. He grabbed Mr Potato Head and made him hop up and down. "You'll never take me alive!" Andy shouted in his best outlaw voice. "Draw!"

Andy let go of Mr Potato Head and grabbed the sheriff. He flipped up the lawman's arm and shouted, "Blam! Blam! Blam!"

"Oof! Ya got me! You no-good sidewinder!" Andy jumped to his feet and clutched Mr Potato Head to his chest. He stumbled round the room, bumping into furniture, doing a long, drawn-out death scene.

Andy's baby sister, Molly, watched from behind bars. Taped to the side of her cot was a cardboard sign with the word JAIL scrawled in crayon.

Andy fell against Molly's crib to catch his breath. With a shrieking giggle, the baby grabbed Mr Potato Head and starting yanking out parts.

"Molly! Give that back!" Andy cried. "He's not

finished dying yet!" As he and his sister played tug-of-war with the toy, Andy bumped into the nightlight.

The nursery lamp wobbled dangerously, then the figurine of Little Bo Peep tumbled head-first towards the floor.

The cowboy's face came alive. He darted a frantic glance at Andy. Good! His back was turned! It wouldn't do for the boy to learn about the toys' ability to come alive.

The sheriff lunged—

Whew! He caught Little Bo Peep an instant before she broke her pretty ceramic neck.

Andy whirled round, grasping his hard-won Mr Potato Head. But as his eyes scanned the room, he didn't even blink. All he saw was his favourite action figure lying stiffly on the bare wood floor. The cowboy's easy grin exactly matched the one the factory had pressed into his plastic face.

Andy grinned. "Good shootin', Woody!" He scooped up the cowboy and yanked the string again.

"*You're my favourite deputy*," Woody said for the four hundred and thirty-seventh time.

Andy galloped into the hall. He propped Woody on the top of the banister—and shoved.

Whooping and shouting, Andy clattered downstairs as Woody slid awkwardly down the banister.

"Gotcha!" Andy cried at the bottom.

3

Then Andy put Woody on his shoulders and romped around the OK Corral, otherwise known as the Davis living room. Together they galloped across the wide-open plains on the bucking bronco Andy's mother called a recliner chair.

"Yeeee-hah!" Andy cried. "Cool!"

When Andy wasn't looking, Woody's face broke into a jawbreaker of a smile. Gosh darn, but it was great being Andy's favourite toy!

Suddenly, Andy's eyes lit up. He tossed Woody on to the couch and ran towards his mother.

Woody landed on his face with his legs skewed in the air. *Hey, what's that all about?* he wondered. The cowboy doll sneaked a peep over the back of the couch.

Woody's usual grin melted like a scoop of ice cream at a Fourth of July picnic. A look of panic spread across his handsome rugged face. This was awful! Terrible! A toy's worst nightmare!

And it was all going to happen . . .

Today!

CHAPTER 2

Colourful helium balloons bobbed on their strings. Crêpe-paper streamers adorned the dining room walls. A jaunty banner draped across the archway proclaimed:

HAPPY BIRTHDAY, ANDY!

Andy batted a blue balloon tied to a dining room chair. "This looks great, Mum!"

"Well," Mrs Davis said, beaming. "I know it's not your birthday but it's better than opening presents on the moving van." She grinned affectionately and ruffled Andy's hair. "Now, go and get Molly. Your friends are going to be here any minute."

"OK, Mum." Andy stopped by the couch to pick up Woody. "Hey, Woody! It's party time!"

Andy pounded up the stairs to his room. As he propped Woody on his bed, he pulled the toy sheriff's string one last time.

"*Somebody's poisoned the waterhole,*" said Woody's pullstring recording.

5

"Come on, Molly." Andy reached into his sister's "jail" and lifted her out. "Ooh, you're getting heavy!" Without looking back, he called out over his shoulder, "See ya later, Woody!"

Slam! Andy kicked the door closed behind him.

Woody shoved his hat back and scratched his forehead, whistling through his teeth as a worried frown creased his brow.

"Pull my string!" he muttered under his breath. "The birthday party's *today*!?" He knew only too well what birthdays meant.

Toys. New toys. And lots of them.

Shiny. Still nice in their boxes with all their parts. Clean.

And full of promise.

Over by the wall a wrestling action figure—tossed down and forgotten—now sprang to life. He pressed his ear to the door, listening as Andy's footsteps faded down the stairs. At last he shot Woody a crooked grin and a thumbs-up sign.

Woody tossed him a salute. "Thanks, Rocky." He hitched up his britches and glanced around the quiet room. "Okay, everybody," he called out. "Coast is clear!"

As usual, there was a moment's pause, like the hesitation of small creatures hiding in the forest. Then a giggle tickled the silence, and a whisper brushed the air.

The toys stirred to life, and the secret magic of Andy's room burst forth like a shaken-up bottle of cola.

Toys rolled out from under the bed, toddled across the floor, bounced out of the toy chest, and flip-flopped down from shelves. Chattering, squeaking, quacking, and ringing, they swarmed into the open terrain of the bedroom floor.

Mr Potato Head wobbled as he sat up on his rounded plastic bottom. He had a blank expression on his face, since all his face parts were strewn around the room.

One by one he jabbed his plastic eyes, ears, nose, and mouth into the small round holes scattered across his body. Then he walked over to Andy's fat pink piggy bank, who was flipping a penny into his coin slot. "Hey, look, Hamm! I'm Picasso!"

The piggy bank stared at Mr Potato Head. His face pieces were all stuck into the wrong holes. Hamm blinked. "Uh . . . I don't get it."

"Ah, you uncultured swine!" Mr Potato Head sighed in disgust as he put his features back where they belonged. He shook his fists at the ceiling. "I'm wasting my best material on these morons!"

High atop Andy's mattress, Woody turned to a plastic green army man standing guard on the bedside table. "Hey, Sarge. Have you seen Slinky?"

"No, sir!" the sergeant said with a stiff salute.

7

"All right, thanks. At ease." Woody leapt off the bed, the spurs of his brown boots jangling when he landed squarely on the floor. "Hey, Slinky!"

A metal *fwump!* sounded under the bed. Two paws shoved a draughts board out from under the hem of the bedspread. Woody's faithful sidekick, a sausage dog with a Slinky toy for a body, wandered out and began setting up the draughts.

"I'm red this time," Slinky said.

Woody sighed. "No, Slink."

"Oh, all right. *You* can be red if you want."

"Not now, Slink!" Woody shook his head. "I've got some bad news."

"Bad news!" Slinky yelped.

Woody shoved a hand over Slinky's mouth and looked round. A few nearby toys inclined their heads, listening for any scrap of hot gossip. Woody led Slinky a few steps away.

"Listen," he whispered. "Just gather everyone up for a staff meeting—and be happy!"

"Got it," said Slinky. He scampered off across the room.

Woody heard a floor-sweeping swish and whirled round. He spotted the tip of a toy snake as it slithered under the bed. Woody bent down and lifted the edge of the spread.

Snake eyes blinked. Beside them, light glinted off the shiny face of a toy robot.

8

"Staff meeting, guys," Woody said firmly. "Your turn for podium duty."

The snake and the robot grumbled and crawled out.

A few paces away the sheriff heard a squeak. He grinned. The knobs were twitching on Etch-A-Sketch, Andy's rectangular drawing toy. "Hey, Etch!" the sheriff called out. "Draw!"

Woody's gun arm shot to his empty holster. Too late.

Etch-A-Sketch had beaten him to the draw. Proudly he displayed the western revolver he'd sketched on his grey screen.

"Got me again, Etch!" Woody teased. "You've been working on that draw. Fastest knobs in the West!" Woody patted him on the corner of his red plastic frame, then walked towards the podium. The snake and the robot were building it out of Legos and Tinker Toys.

Woody nodded his approval. The meeting would start soon. He'd better make a list.

"Now, where is that . . . hey! Who moved my doodle pad way over here?" He walked over and picked up the tablet.

Suddenly, behind him—

"*Roaaaarrrr!*"

Woody casually turned around. "Oh, how ya doin', Rex?"

9

A not-very-ferocious-looking plastic tyrannosaurus smiled hopefully, his tiny claws clutched to his chest. "Did I scare you, Woody? Did I? Tell me the truth?"

Woody bit his lip and cleared his throat. "Well," he said diplomatically, "I was *close* to being scared that time."

Rex sighed and followed Woody towards the podium. "I'm going for fearsome here," he mumbled, shaking his scaly head. "But I just don't feel it. I think I'm just coming off as annoying . . ."

Woody started to comment, but a shepherd's crook suddenly hooked him around the waist. One big yank and he found himself nose to nose with a smiling Little Bo Peep. "Oh, uh . . . hi, Bo."

The slender figurine batted her blue eyes. "I wanted to thank you, Woody!" she drawled. "For saving me."

Woody blushed. "Oh, hey—it was nothing."

Bo Peep smiled sweetly. "What do you say I get someone else to watch the sheep tonight, hmmm?"

Woody gulped.

Bo gestured with her crook towards the alphabet blocks that decorated the base of her lamp. "Remember," she added, "I'm just a couple of blocks away." With a pert little wave, she sashayed over towards the podium, then sank gracefully to the floor, smoothing out her long pink polka-dot skirts.

Woody's heart *boinged* like a jack-in-the-box. He

shook his head to clear it and glanced round. *Gosh darn*, he thought sheepishly, tugging on the red bandanna he wore round his neck. *Hope nobody saw that!*

All business again, he scribbled some notes on his doodle pad and strode towards the podium.

Slinky was busy herding all the toys into place. "Come on, come on! Smaller toys up front!"

Everyone crowded around expectantly as Woody took his place on the podium. A toy tape recorder waddled up beside him.

"Oh, thanks, Mike," Woody said. He picked up Mike's microphone and blew. "Hello? Testing, testing. Can everybody hear me? Great."

He glanced down at the notes on his doodle pad.

"Okay. First item today. Has everyone picked a moving buddy?"

All the toys began talking at once.

"I didn't know we were supposed to have one already," Rex whined.

"Hey, Woody!" Mr Potato Head held up one of his plastic arms. "Do we have to hold hands?"

The toys nudged one another and laughed.

Woody shook his head. "Oh, yeah. You guys think this is a big joke. But listen—we've only got one week left before the big move. I don't want *any* toys left behind. A moving buddy—if you don't have one, *get* one!"

11

Woody looked back at his doodle pad. "All right, next on the list . . . oh, yeah. Tuesday night's 'Plastic Corrosion Awareness' meeting was a big success, and we want to thank Mr Spell for putting that on for us. Thanks, Mr Spell."

"You are welcome," Mr Spell droned.

Woody stared at his list. He flipped the page, hoping some new topic would magically be written there. But the page was as blank as his mind.

Gosh darn, he hated this part of the job. But he was the sheriff. Andy's favourite toy. He enjoyed the privileges; he had to accept the responsibilities, too.

There was no use putting it off any longer. He had bad news. The toys would have to be told.

CHAPTER 3

"Um. Oh, yes. One more thing, a minor note here." Woody's voice dropped to a whisper as soft as a spring breeze sighing across the prairie. "Andy's birthday party has been moved up to today." He coughed and shouted, "AND NEXT WE HAVE—"

The room exploded into squeaks, squeals, bells, barks, and whistles.

"Wait a minute! Hold the phone!" Mr Potato Head yelled from the back row. "What do you mean, the party's *today*? Andy's birthday is not till next week!"

Woody held up his hands. "Now, now. Obviously Andy's mum wanted to have the party before the move. *I'm* not worried. *You* shouldn't be worried."

Mr Potato Head elbowed his way to the front of the crowd, glaring at the sheriff. "Of course Woody ain't worried!" he cried. "He's been Andy's favourite since kindergarten!"

Some of the toys mumbled their agreement.

Woody felt as if he'd been slapped.

"Hey, come on, Mr Potato Head," Slinky responded, speaking up for his pal. "If Woody says it's all right, then, well, darn it, it's good enough for me. Woody has never steered us wrong before."

Woody jumped down from the podium and walked through the crowd, looking each toy straight in the eye. "Listen, everybody," he said with emotion. "It doesn't matter how much Andy plays with us. What matters is that we're here for Andy when he needs us. *That's* what we're made for. Right?"

One by one the whirring, muttering, chiming toys fell silent. Ashamed, they stared at their feet . . . or paws or wheels . . . or whatever.

It wasn't easy being a toy. Especially on days like today. But Andy Davis was a good kid. He was kind to them . . . most of the time. And they loved him with all their hearts. Woody was right. That was the most important thing.

Hamm the piggy bank broke the silence. "Uh, pardon me," he said from the windowsill. "I hate to break up the staff meeting. But . . .

"THEY'RE HERE! BIRTHDAY GUESTS AT THREE O'CLOCK!"

The peaceful bedroom erupted into chaos! Woody held up his hands. "Stay calm, everybody!" he shouted with authority. "Stay—"

CRUNCH!

Too late. Like a herd of stampeding cattle, the toys bolted towards the bedroom window.

Woody, lying crumpled on the floor, spat out a mouthful of dust, propped himself up on one elbow, and announced, "Uh, meeting adjourned."

No one heard him. They were already plastered to the window pane, packing the windowsill tighter than a toy shop shelf at Christmas.

Hamm gulped as he stared down into the front yard. "Oh, boy. Will ya take a look at all those presents?"

"I can't see a thing!" Mr Potato Head complained impatiently. He pulled his eyes out of his head and held them up above the crowd.

He and the other toys stared down in horror.

On the street below, kids sprang from their parents' cars, each carrying an object that struck terror into the hearts of Andy's toys.

A birthday present.

Hamm shook his head. "Yesiree, we're next month's garage sale fodder for sure."

"Any dinosaur-shaped ones?" Rex asked worriedly.

"Ah, for crying out loud," Hamm jeered. "They're all in boxes, you idiot!"

Rex said nervously, "The presents—th-they're getting bigger!"

15

"Wait!" said Slinky. "There's a nice little one over there."

He pointed at a boy who was facing away from the window. Only the tiny tip of a present showed. Then the boy turned. The present was over four feet long!

"AAAAAHHHH!!!" screamed the toys.

"We're doomed!" Rex howled.

"SPELL THE WORD DUSTBIN," Mr Spell droned.

The toys began to wail and moan.

Woody sighed. Things were getting out of control. He had to do something—fast—or he'd have a serious problem on his hands. "All right! All right!" he called out.

The toys turned and faced him, and Woody's heart lurched in his chest. Never had he seen the faces of playthings so twisted in fear. The worn and faded toys had the saddest looks of all.

Woody sighed and smiled affectionately at his friends. "If I send out the troops, will you all calm down?"

"Yes! Yes! We promise!" Rex cried.

Woody the lawman was back in charge. His boots rang out against the wooden floorboards as he strode purposefully towards the nightstand. "Sergeant!" he shouted up to the tabletop. "Establish a recon post downstairs. Code Red. You know what to do."

"YES, SIR!" the little green army man replied.

16

He shimmied down one leg of the nightstand, then dashed to the corner, where a plastic container labelled BUCKET O' SOLDIERS lay on its side.

Sarge yanked off the lid. "All right, men!" he barked into the bucket. "You heard him. Code Red. Repeat. We are at Code Red! Let's move move move move!"

One by one the plastic soldiers marched out of their bucket barracks.

CHAPTER 4

reaaak . . . Andy's bedroom door eased open. A single green army scout crept out into the upstairs hall, scoping for any signs of danger.

Satisfied that the coast was clear, he signalled his troops. Dozens of soldiers streamed forward, carefully transporting the specialized equipment they needed for their intelligence mission.

A skipping rope and a baby monitor.

The soldiers darted behind the railings of the banister and held their position. Sarge surveyed their route through binoculars.

Suddenly he jerked back, melting into the shadows and signalling *danger*! to his men.

Directly below them, Mrs Davis walked by.

The soldiers froze into green plastic position, secretly monitoring the enemy's movements. As soon as Mrs Davis moved out of range, Sarge signalled his men to proceed with the mission.

Paratroopers crept to the edge of the landing, then

bravely leapt off. *Fwump!* Well-packed parachutes opened perfectly to carry them safely to the polished wood floor below.

After a quick look round, they signalled to the soldiers who remained waiting above. All clear!

Seconds later Andy's skipping rope snaked down from above. More soldiers abseiled to the floor.

The troops fell in and marched towards the living room. Suddenly a door opened. They heard footsteps. Again, they froze into their various premoulded poses . . .

Just as Mrs Davis came through the door and stomped down in the middle of the squad.

"What in the world—?" She frowned at the toy army men scattered across the floor and shook her head. "I thought I told Andy to put these away."

But with Andy's party in full swing, Mrs Davis was too busy to stop and pick up toys. With the toe of her shoe, she simply swept the army men out of the way.

As soon as she was gone, Sarge signalled to the handful of men still waiting above on the stairs. Carefully they lowered themselves down the skipping rope, riding on top of the baby monitor. When they reached the floor, they quickly dragged the monitor towards a potted plant.

Sarge started to follow but then noticed that one of his men had been injured.

Holding his leg, the soldier waved for his commander to keep moving. "Go on without me!"

But Sarge would have none of that. "A good soldier never leaves a man behind," he instructed as he helped the injured soldier to his feet.

Suddenly Sarge put a finger to his lips and cocked his head.

Footsteps! Lots of them.

Coming this way!

The injured soldier choked down his moans of pain as Sarge dragged him towards the living room. Exhausted, the two comrades stumbled to take cover behind the potted plant just as the first pair of feet stomped past.

As a medic examined the soldier, the rest of the crew quickly set up the baby monitor. Sarge scanned the horizon with his binoculars. Suddenly his face brightened.

On the Davises' living room coffee table a tower of gift-wrapped packages loomed ominously towards the ceiling. Sarge whistled softly through his teeth. *Man, what a haul!*

Sarge leaned into the baby monitor. *"Attention, Mother Bird. This is Alpha Bravo."*

Upstairs in Andy's room, Woody and his friends clustered around the receiver. "This is it!" Woody cried excitedly. "Shhh! Quiet, everybody!"

Sarge's deep voice came through loud and clear. *"Andy's opening the first present now."*

Mr Potato Head crossed his fingers and chanted in the suspenseful silence: *"Mrs* Potato Head . . . *Mrs* Potato Head . . ."

Rex shot him a weird look.

"Hey, I can dream, can't I?"

"SHHHHHHHHH!"

"The bow's coming off," Sarge's voice reported through the monitor. *"Andy's ripping off the wrapping paper. . . . It's . . . it's . . ."*

The toys held their breath.

"It's a lunch box!" Sarge announced. *"Repeat: We've got a lunch box here!"*

"Hoo-whee!" Woody howled gleefully, slapping his hat against his jeans. "A lunch box!"

The toys clapped and cheered.

"Okay," came Sarge's voice. *"Next present."*

The toys hushed and leaned forwards expectantly.

"Hmm, it appears to be . . . uh, bedsheets."

"Who invited *that* kid?" Mr Potato Head wondered sarcastically.

But bedsheets got another round of cheers from Andy's toys.

One by one Sarge reported on each present as Andy unwrapped it. Each time it was good news! Slowly the toys began to relax a little.

Woody rubbed his chin. *Dang, these kids are a mite*

loco if you ask me, he thought. *Where are all the toys? Hey, maybe their mums brought the presents!* Woody grinned. *Who cares?* he thought. It was turning out to be their lucky day after all.

"*Okay*," Sarge announced at last. "*We're on the very last present. It's a big one. . . .*"

The toys who had fingers crossed them. Every stuffed, plastic, and wooden head leaned forwards. Time crawled.

Finally Sarge revealed: "*It's . . . it's a board game! Repeat. Battleships, the board game.*"

Some of the toys stamped and cheered. Others hugged and cried tears of joy and relief. Yes, it was a toy—but one they could all live with.

"All right!" Hamm shouted. He pounded Mr Potato Head on the back so hard, his face parts flew off.

"Hey, watch it!"

"Sorry about that, old Spudhead."

"So, what did I tell you? Huh? Nothing to worry about," Woody cried out.

Slinky yipped happily. "I knew you were right, Woody. I never doubted you for a second."

Downstairs, plantside, Sarge congratulated his men. "Mission accomplished. Well done, soldiers. Pack it up—we're going home."

"Wait a minute!"

22

The sound of Mrs Davis' voice stopped Sarge in his tracks. "Halt!" he hissed to his men.

Sarge winced. He had forgotten one of his own rules. The most important one: When dealing with humans, always expect the unexpected.

Sarge watched, sweating, as Mrs Davis jumped up and hurried to the coat cupboard by the front door. She tossed a teasing look over her shoulder, then squealed, "Ooooh, what have we got here?"

"Quick!" Sarge ordered, pointing at the baby monitor. "Turn that thing back on!"

A soldier rammed the switch.

"Come in, Mother Bird!" Sarge said frantically. *"Urgent! Mum has pulled a surprise present from the cupboard. Andy's opening it. He's really excited! It's a huge package. Oh, wait. One of the kids is in the way. I can't see."*

At last the kid moved out of the way.

Sarge blinked.

"Uh-oh. It's a . . . oh, my!"

Sarge and his soldiers stared open-mouthed at the unwrapped present as the kids screamed in delight.

It was worse than any of the toys could have imagined.

pstairs in Andy's room, the rest of the toys
waited, hearts pounding.

Rex grabbed a leg of the nightstand and
shook it in frustration. "It's a what? *What is it?*"

The monitor fell off the shaking table and tumbled to the ground. *Thwack!*

A small plastic rectangle fell off the back. Batteries rolled out across the floor.

"Oh no!" Rex gasped.

"Oooh! You big lizard!" Mr Potato Head shouted. "Now we'll never know what it is!"

"Yeah, way to go," Hamm added.

All the toys were shouting. Mr Potato Head pounced on the batteries and fumbled as he tried to stick them back into the monitor.

"No, no! Turn 'em round!" Woody shouted.

"You're putting them in backwards!" Hamm cried.

Woody leapt down from the bed. "Plus is positive, minus is negative—oh, let me do it!"

Woody shoved Hamm and Mr Potato Head aside. He grabbed a battery and jammed it in the right way. As soon as he snapped the second one in, Sarge's voice crackled urgently across the room:

"*Red alert! Andy is coming upstairs! Juvenile intrusion. Repeat! Resume your positions now!*"

"Andy's coming!" Woody shouted. "Everybody— back to your places. Hurry!"

The toys scattered like frightened mice.

"Where's my ear?" Mr Potato Head cried, scrambling across the floor. "Do you see my ear?"

Splat! Rex smashed into a bookshelf as the sound of pounding footsteps came closer and closer.

Woody leapt—

The door banged open.

The sheriff fell limp in his special spot on the bed just as Andy and his friends charged in.

The kids were all jabbering at once.

"Hey, Andy, can I see it."

"Wow! Cool! Look at those wings. Are they on springs or something?"

"Look at his laser light up. *Choom! Choom!*"

"Take that, Zurg!" Andy cried.

Woody sneaked a look from the corner of his eye, trying desperately to see what they were talking

25

about. But there were too many kids in the way. He couldn't see a thing.

Then a mob of kids pounced on Andy's bed.

Woody felt himself being shoved out of the way. He clutched at the bedspread, trying to hang on. But it was no use. Slowly he slumped to the floor behind the bed.

His heart sank to the toes of his boots. It didn't take chicken brains to work out what was going on here.

No doubt about it.

A brand-new toy had arrived.

CHAPTER 6

"Quick!" one of Andy's friends said. "Make a space! This is where his spaceship lands. CRASH!"

"And look," Andy said. "You press his back and he does a karate chop."

Woody lay beneath the bed as he listened to Andy and his friends chatter. He felt sick to his stomach.

Get a grip! he scolded himself. He had to be strong, stronger than the average toy. It would be up to him—as sheriff and favourite toy—to keep up morale. *Shoot!* If only he could see what was causing all this fuss!

Unexpectedly Mrs Davis came to Woody's rescue. An-dy!" she called up the stairs. "Come on down. It's time for games. And we've got lots of prizes!"

"Oh, yeah," Andy said. "Come on guys!" He ushered his pack of noisy friends out of the room.

The door slammed shut.

Slowly, cautiously, Andy's toys came to life and

crept towards the boy's head. This new thing that Andy got—it was still in the room!

"What is it?"

"What's up there?"

"Woody?" Rex hissed. "Who's up there with you?"

Sneezing from the dust, Woody crawled out from under the bed.

The toys gasped in shock.

"Woody!" Slinky cried. "What are you doing under *there*?"

Woody pulled himself to his feet and slapped the dust from his jeans. "Uhh . . . nothing. I'm fine." He pasted a big sunny smile on his face as he fought the desire to tug on his neckerchief. "I'm sure Andy was just a little excited, that's all. Too much cake and ice cream, I suppose. It's just a mistake."

"Well," Mr Potato Head said sarcastically, "that 'mistake' is sitting in *your* spot!"

Rex gasped. "Woody—have you been replaced?"

Woody slung his arm around the dinosaur's narrow shoulders. "Hey! What did I tell you earlier? *No one* is getting replaced."

But the other toys weren't so sure.

"Now," Woody continued, "let's all be polite and give whatever it is up there a nice big 'Andy's room' welcome. Okay? Come on."

Woody smiled confidently—and fought down the

28

butterflies brawling in the pit of his stomach. He inched his way up the side of the bed. He'd be the first to lay eyes on this new toy. Who knew what he'd see?

Late-afternoon sunlight streamed in through the window, momentarily robbing his eyes of sight. He blinked and began to make out a dark silhouette standing tall against the light.

And then he could see. "Hooo-wheee . . ."

A toy man—unlike any Woody had ever seen—stood boldly in the centre of Andy's bed.

He wore a white high-tech spacesuit, hinged for ease of movement. A green control panel studded with a complex array of push buttons, stickers, and lights covered the top half of his broad chest. A clear plastic bubble the size and shape of a punch bowl shielded his head, leaving plenty of breathing room. Through this clear helmet Woody could see the arched brow, keen eyes, and strong chin of a confident explorer.

As Woody gawked, the stranger came to life and pressed a blue button on the right side of his chest.

Bleep! Bleep!

"Buzz Lightyear to Star Command. Come in, Star Command." The man paused for an answer.

No response.

"Star Command," he repeated more forcefully. "Do you read me?" His mouth tightened into a stiff grimace. "Why don't they answer?"

He took a step, then something caught his eye.

Woody followed the new toy's gaze. Buzz was staring at the smashed toy box in which he had been packaged.

"My ship!" he cried. He ran to the crumpled box to examine the damage, then stamped one space-booted foot. "Darn! This will take weeks to repair!"

Fuming, he flipped open a plastic communications device strapped to his arm. "Buzz Lightyear Mission Log. Stardate 4072: My ship has run off course en route to sector twelve. I've crash-landed on a strange planet. The impact must have awakened me from hypersleep."

Buzz bounced up and down on the squishy surface of the bed. "Terrain seems a bit unstable," he reported into his communicator. "No readout yet on whether the air is breathable." He glanced around. "And there seems to be no sign of intelligent life anywhere."

Woody poked his head in front of Buzz. "Hello?"

"HA-YAAAAAHH!" Buzz jumped back, arms raised in a defensive stance.

Woody threw up his hands like a holdup victim. "Whoa! Did I frighten you? Sorry. Didn't mean to." He slowly lowered his right hand and held it out to the stranger. "Howdy! My name is Woody, and this is Andy's room. Oh, and, um . . . also, there's been a bit of a mix-up. You see, this is *my* spot, the bed here—"

"Local law enforcement!" Buzz interrupted, nodding at Woody's badge. "It's about time you got here. I'm Buzz Lightyear, space ranger, Universe Protection Unit. My ship crash-landed here by mistake."

"Yeah, it is a mistake," Woody agreed, "because you see, the bed, here . . . this is my spot."

But Buzz didn't seem to hear. He strode away, scanning the terrain of what he thought was a strange new planet. Woody hurried to keep up.

"I need to repair my turbo boosters," Buzz informed the sheriff. "Do you people still use fossil fuels? Or have you discovered crystallic fusion?"

Woody took off his cowboy hat and scratched his head. "Well, let's see, we've got double-A batteries—"

Suddenly Buzz yanked Woody flat down on the bed. "Halt!" he cried. "Who goes there?"

Andy's toys were crawling up over the edge of the bed.

"Don't shoot!" Rex the dinosaur yelled out. "It's okay! We're friends!"

Buzz cocked his head towards Woody. "Sheriff, do you know these life-forms?"

"Yes," Woody replied. "They're Andy's toys."

Buzz seemed to relax. "Okay, everyone. You're clear to come up." He stood and walked over to the toys. "Greetings! I am Buzz Lightyear," he said boldly. "I come in peace."

Rex rushed up and grabbed his hand, pumping it up and down with enthusiasm. "Oh, I'm so glad you're not a dinosaur!"

"Why, uh, thank you," Buzz said, a puzzled look on his face. "Thank you all for your kind welcome."

Rex stared at the panel of buttons on the chest of Buzz's spacesuit. "Say, what's *that* button do?"

"I'll show you." Buzz pressed the button. A clear, bold prerecorded voice cried out. "*Buzz Lightyear to the rescue!*"

"Ooooooh!" the toys murmured.

"Hey," said Slinky. "Woody's got something like that. His is a pullstring, only—"

"Only it sounds like a car ran over it," Mr Potato Head joked.

"Yeah, not like yours," Hamm said with admiration. "Yours is a high-quality sound system. Probably all copper wiring, huh? So, where are you from? Singapore? Hong Kong?"

Buzz stared at the piggy bank, one eyebrow raised. "Well, no. Actually, I'm stationed up in the gamma quadrant of sector four. As a member of the elite Universe Protection Unit of the Space Ranger Corps, I protect the galaxy from the threat of invasion from the Evil Emperor Zurg, sworn enemy of the Galactic Alliance."

You could have heard a pin drop.

"Oh, really?" Mr Potato Head said firmly. "I'm from PlaySkool."

Frowning, Woody glanced at Buzz's box. On one side he could see a drawing of Buzz Lightyear. Printed in a cartoon balloon coming out of his mouth was the exact same speech he'd just given!

Woody snorted and walked over to Bo Peep. He crossed his arms and forced a casual smile. "Huh! You'd think they'd never seen a new toy before."

"Well, sure." Bo shrugged. "Just look at him. He's got more gadgets than a Swiss Army knife!"

Andy's toys crowded round the newcomer as if he were a movie star. The robot shyly poked a finger towards a large red button on Buzz's upper arm.

"Ah, ah, ah!" Buzz warned, shaking his index finger like a fussy schoolteacher. "Please be careful. You don't want to be in the way when my laser goes off."

"A laser!" Mr Potato Head exclaimed. He shot Woody a mischievious look. "Hey, Woody—how come *you* don't have a laser?"

"It's not a laser! It's a dinky little lightbulb that blinks!" Woody was usually pretty easygoing, but he was getting a little irked by all this fuss over Buzz. "Look, we're all impressed with Andy's new toy, but—"

"Toy?" Buzz exclaimed scornfully.

Woody nodded with a smug smile. "T-O-Y. Toy."

"Excuse me," Buzz said firmly. "I think the word you're searching for is *space ranger*."

"The word I'm searching for I can't say because there are preschool toys present!"

Mr Potato Head chortled. "Getting kind of tense, aren't you, Sheriff?"

"Mr Lightyear?" Rex asked shyly. "What does a space ranger do, exactly?"

Woody rolled his eyes. He couldn't believe it!" He's not a space ranger! He doesn't *really* fight evil or shoot lasers or fly or—"

"Excuse me." Buzz calmly pressed a button on his chest. An outrageous pair of high-tech wings sprang open on the back of his spacesuit.

"WOW!"

"Look at *that*!"

"Oh, what? *What!?*" Woody couldn't believe how gullible his friends were. They were falling for this guy's cheap bells and whistles like a crowd at a carnival sideshow.

He grabbed hold of one of Buzz's wings. "Look! These are plastic, for gosh sakes. He can't really fly!"

Buzz raised his chin proudly. "Excuse me. These wings are terillium-carbonic alloy. And I *can* fly."

Woody shook his head. "No, you can't."

"*Yes* I can."

"You can't."

"Can."

"Can't! Can't! *Can't!*"

Buzz's eyes flashed angrily. "I tell you, I could fly around this room with my eyes closed!"

Woody's eyes lit up. Now he had him! This bragging chunk of fancy plastic was going to hang himself. "Okay, then, *buster*. Prove it!"

"All right, I will!" Buzz strode towards the edge of Andy's bed. "Stand back, everyone!" he warned as he struck a dramatic pose, arms akimbo. "To infinity and beyond!" He raised his arms and jumped.

Woody grinned and waited for the *crunch*! Bye-bye, brand-new birthday toy! Hello, dents and scratches!

Boing!

Boing? Woody dashed to the edge and looked down.

Then up.

He couldn't believe it! Buzz had landed on a big rubber ball and bounced! When he plunged back down, he landed on a Hot Wheels car, went zooming down the track, swooshed through a show-stopping loop-the-loop, then flew out of the car . . .

Towards a mobile. He grabbed on and swung around as easily as a gymnast, then let go . . .

Flipped in the air . . .

And landed firmly on the bed—right in front of Woody's nose.

"*Can.*"

Woody couldn't believe the toy's dumb luck! But the sheriff seemed to be the only one who saw what had really happened. His friends were nearly drooling in admiration.

"Wow!" Rex crooned. "You flew magnificently!"

Bo Peep winked. "I think I found my moving buddy."

Buzz smiled modestly. "Why, thank you. Thank you all."

"That wasn't flying," Woody muttered. "That was falling with style." He scuffed his boot at a loose thread on the bedspread. "In a couple of days, everything will be just the way it was before. They'll see. I'm still Andy's favourite toy."

CHAPTER 7

The next morning Woody woke up stiff and sore. Darkness surrounded him. For a moment he couldn't remember where he was.

Then it all came back to him. *Arrrgh*! He was angry enough to spit nails.

Woody had just gone through the worst night of his life. He'd done something he'd never done before.

He'd slept in the toy box.

How humiliating! He'd always slept on Andy's bed.

He pushed up the lid and peeped out. All clear.

He leaped from the toy chest and took a deep breath of fresh air. He reached up to adjust his hat and discovered it was missing.

A rubber shark popped up from the chest behind him, wearing Woody's hat.

"Look! I'm a cowboy! Howdy! Howdy! Howdy!" he shouted.

Disgusted, the sheriff grabbed his hat and jammed it onto his head, slamming the toy chest lid.

Then Woody spotted something that really shocked him.

Across the room Buzz was already up, surrounded by adoring fans. No wonder he looked so good. He had slept on Andy's bed!

"It looks as though I've been accepted into your culture," Buzz told Rex and Slinky. "Look."

Buzz raised his foot so they could see the sole of his shiny white spaceboot. The name ANDY was neatly printed in bold letters with a permanent marker. "See? Your chief, Andy, inscribed his name on me."

Woody gulped. He bent over and looked at the bottom of his dusty, worn cowboy boot. The name ANDY was written there, too. But in a childish scrawl. And the letters had begun to fade.

"Don't let it get you down," a gentle voice said.

Woody quickly dropped his foot and looked up.

Little Bo Peep was smiling at him—something that usually made his heart do cartwheels. But today her smile looked different somehow. Today it was tinged with pity.

"Hey," Woody said, smiling, trying to act nonchalant. "Get what? Down where?"

"So what if Andy's excited by Buzz?" Bo said. "He'll always have a special place for you."

"Yeah," Mr Potato Head cracked as he sauntered past. "Like in the attic."

"All right! That's it!" Woody growled. He'd had enough of being pushed around and shoved aside. It was time to deal with this trespasser head-on.

Buzz Lightyear had his cardboard box "spaceship" up on blocks. He lay down on a skateboard, then rolled himself beneath it to do repairs. The snake and the robot hovered nearby, eager to be of service to their new hero.

"Unidirectional bonding strip!" Buzz barked, holding out his hand.

The robot turned to the snake. "More tape!"

But Woody stepped between them and pulled Buzz out from under the spaceship. He glared into the surprised spaceman's face. "Listen, Lightsnack. You stay away from Andy. He's mine, and no one's taking him away from me."

"What *are* you talking about?" Buzz shook his head impatiently, then turned to the robot. "Where's that bonding strip?" He rolled himself back under.

Woody hauled him right back out.

"And another thing. Stop with this 'spaceman' business. It's getting on my nerves."

Buzz sighed irritably and stood up. "Are you saying you want to lodge a complaint with Star Command?"

"Oh, so you want to do it the hard way, huh?"

"Don't even think about it, cowboy."

"Oh, yeah, tough guy?"

Woody poked Buzz in the chest—and accidentally jabbed a green button. Buzz's helmet *whooshed* open.

"AAGGGHHH!" Buzz clutched his throat, gasping for air. He dropped to his knees, then toppled over on his side, writhing on the ground, holding his breath. Soon he was turning a little blue.

The robot and Slinky looked at each other nervously. Woody just rolled his eyes.

Finally, against his will, Buzz was forced to suck in a huge rasping gasp of breath.

He waited a moment. Blinked. Sniffed.

Then exhaled.

Nothing happened.

Buzz seemed stunned. "The air isn't toxic!" he said in wonderment.

Then he turned on Woody. "How dare you open a spaceman's helmet on an uncharted planet! My eyeballs could have been sucked from their sockets!" Glaring, he *whooshed* his helmet closed.

"Wait a minute," Woody said. "Don't tell me. You actually *believe* you're the Buzz Lightyear?"

Buzz just sniffed, as if insulted.

"Geesh, all this time I thought it was an act!" Woody turned to the other toys, who were gathering round. "Hey, guys! Look!" he said sarcastically. "It's the *real* Buzz Lightyear!"

Buzz cleared his throat, then blinked a couple of times. "You're . . . mocking me, aren't you?"

Woody guffawed "No, no, no, no." Then he croaked, staring over Buzz's shoulder, his face twisted in horror. "Buzz! L-look! An alien!"

Buzz whirled around. "Where? Where?"

"*Sucker!*" Woody clutched his stomach as he burst out laughing again.

A dog barked, somewhere outside. Woody's laughter died in his throat. Every toy froze.

Laughter floated in through the open window.

"It's Sid!" Slinky whispered.

Rex looked frightened. "I thought he was at summer camp."

"They must have kicked him out early this summer," Hamm grumbled.

Buzz watched, confused, as the toys seemed drawn to the window, almost against their will.

"Who is it this time?" Mr Potato Head asked.

Woody pulled himself up on the windowsill and shook his head. "I can't tell. Where's Lenny?"

A windup set of binoculars waddled over. Woody picked the toy up and looked through him to survey the yard.

A boy was playing in his messy fenced-in back-yard. The grungy skull-and-crossbones T-shirt he wore was torn. His mangy dog was digging holes.

This boy was not like Andy. There was something mean about him. Something that made him cruel.

The boy was taunting a miserable-looking toy soldier as he strapped a huge M-80 to his back with masking tape. The boy laughed as he lit the fuse.

"Oh no," Woody moaned. "It's a Combat Carl."

Buzz broke through the crowd and made his way to the windowsill. "What's going on, Sheriff?"

"Nothing that concerns you, spaceman," Woody said tersely. "Just us *toys*."

"I'd better take a look anyway." Buzz grabbed Lenny from Woody's hands and surveyed the scene. Then his mouth fell open. "Why is that soldier strapped to an explosive device?"

Woody steered the binoculars till Buzz could see the boy. "That's why. Sid Phillips."

"You mean that happy child?"

"That ain't no happy child," Mr Potato Head snapped.

"He tortures toys," Rex said. "Just for fun!"

"Well, then, we've got to do something." Buzz stepped out onto the window ledge.

"What are you doing?" Bo Peep exclaimed, grabbing his arm. "Get down!"

Buzz pulled away. "I'm going to go down there and teach that boy a lesson!"

"Yeah, sure," Woody mocked. "You go ahead.

Oooh! Melt him with your scary laser." He poked at Buzz's control panel, making it beep.

"Hey, be careful with that!" Buzz said. "It's extremely dangerous."

Lenny saw that the fuse on the explosive had almost burned down. "Hit the dirt!" he cried.

The toys scattered, shrieking.

BOOM! Ba-ba-BOOM!

Woody and Buzz were thrown to the floor. They could hear bits and pieces of toy sharpnel pelting the side of Andy's house. Then silence. In that silence they could hear Sid laughing.

"Yes! He's history! Did you see that, Scud? Oh, that was so sweet!"

Slowly the toys rose from their hiding places and crept back to the window.

Scud the dog ran towards a shallow crater in the yard. He grabbed what was left of Combat Carl in his vicious teeth.

The toys cringed and turned away.

"I could have stopped him," Buzz said quietly.

"Buzz, I'd love to see you try," Woody replied. "Of course, I'd love to see you as a crater."

But it was Bo Peep who spoke for them all, "The sooner we move away from this house the better."

CHAPTER 8

A few days later Andy and his mum had been packing all day for their big move, but now they were taking a break. She was taking Andy to his favourite restaurant, Pizza Planet, one last time before the move. She had told Andy he could bring a toy. But only one.

Moment of truth! Woody thought. He grabbed the Magic 8 Ball—it was supposed to tell your future—and shook it. Hard.

"Will Andy pick me?" Woody whispered to the Magic 8 Ball. He turned it over, and his future was revealed: DON'T COUNT ON IT.

Woody threw down the ball in disgust. *Rubbish!* he thought as he watched the ball roll off behind the desk with a loud thud.

Hmmm. He sneaked a look at Buzz, who was standing a few paces away on Andy's desk. Then he peered down into the narrow space between the desk and the wall. It was dark and deep and laced with cobwebs. The Magic 8 Ball was wedged near the bottom.

Andy's radio-controlled racing car was parked at the other end of the desk. And its nose was pointed directly at that silly spaceman. Woody grinned.

"Oh, Buzz! Buzz Lightyear!" Woody called as he ran over. "Thank goodness! We've got trouble."

"Trouble? Where?"

Woody led him to the edge of the desk. "Down there. A helpless toy is *trapped*, Buzz!"

"Then we have no time to lose." Buzz stared into the shadowy ravine. "I can't see anything."

"Oh, he's there," Woody assured him. "Just keep looking." Smothering a snigger, Woody backed up and grabbed the remote control, then flipped a switch. The car's headlights flicked on like gleaming eyes. The motor hummed.

And then . . . Woody almost changed his mind. He'd always been the good guy in this town. He'd always stood for honesty and decency. Then this Buzz Lightyear came and changed everything.

Still, Woody hestitated, torn. He *almost* put down the remote. But then he saw the afternoon sunlight glinting off Buzz Lightyear's gleaming white space suit.

Jealousy squeezed Woody's heart into a tight green wad. Nothing about Woody gleamed—not even his tarnished star.

Woody squeezed the remote.

The car zoomed forwards.

Buzz spun round. With a gasp, he leapt out of the way.

The car struck a notice board on the wall, and pins rained down like shrapnel.

The bulletin board fell and knocked over Andy's globe. The globe rolled towards Buzz, who dashed across the desk—and at last jumped out of the way. Gasping for breath, Buzz looked round and spotted Woody holding the remote.

Woody caught Buzz's eye and dropped the control. But just then the rolling globe struck Andy's folding-arm desk lamp. The lamp swung round in a wide arc. Woody jumped aside. But it whacked Buzz through the open window.

"Buzz!" Rex shrieked.

Startled, many of the toys, who hadn't seen what happened, rushed to the window.

Woody crouched on the ledge on his hands and knees, staring down into the yard. "Buzz!" he shouted. But there was no sign of him anywhere.

"I don't see him in the drive." Slinky sounded worried. "Maybe he bounced into Sid's yard."

Woody gulped and began to back away.

Over on the desk the car began to whirr.

"What is it, boy?" Rex asked.

"Whirrrr! Whirrrr! Whirrr!"

Mr Potato Head nodded knowingly. "He's saying that was no accident."

"What do you mean?" Bo Peep asked.

"I mean Humpty Dumpty was pushed"—he glared at the sheriff—"by Woody!"

"Wait a minute," Woody said. "You don't think I *meant* to knock Buzz out the window, do you Potato Head?"

"That's *Mr* Potato Head to you—you murderer!"

"It was an accident!" Woody exclaimed. "Come on, guys. You've got to believe me."

Sarge popped out of his bucket. "Where is your honour, dirtbag? You don't deserve to—"

Woody slammed the lid back on and sat on it.

Mr Potato Head circled Woody like a prosecutor in a court of law. "Couldn't handle Buzz cutting in on your playtime, could you, Woody? Didn't want to face the fact that Buzz just might be Andy's new favourite toy, so you got rid of him. Well, what if Andy starts playing with me more, huh, Woody? You gonna knock me out of the window, too?"

Hamm stepped up beside Mr Potato Head. "I don't think we should give him the chance."

Suddenly Sarge shoved the lid off the Bucket o' Soldiers. "There he is, men! Get him!"

The soldiers surrounded Woody. Potato Head, Rocky, and Hamm grabbed his arms.

"Wait!" Woody cried. "I can explain everything."

"Hey, leave him alone!" Slinky barked loyally.

But no one was listening any more.

"I say string him up by his pullstring!" Mr Potato Head shouted.

Suddenly they heard Andy just outside the door. "Okay, Mum, be right down. I've got to get Buzz."

The startled lynch mob dropped Woody and ran to their usual places. Quickly they congealed into their shop-bought expressions and poses.

Andy came in and dashed to his desk. Then he stopped, puzzled. He pulled out his chair and looked round. He got down on his knees and searched the floor. "Hey, Mum!" he shouted. "Do you know where Buzz is?"

"Pssst!" Mr Potato Head hissed at Woody.

Barely moving, Woody slanted a look. Over in a corner Mr Potato Head held up Etch-A-Sketch— with a hangman's noose sketched on the screen.

Woody gulped.

"Andy!" Mrs Davis shouted upstairs. "I'm heading through the door!"

"But, Mum, I can't find Buzz!"

"Well, honey, just grab some other toy. Now, come on!"

"Okay . . ." Disappointed, Andy looked round. He spotted Woody lying on the desktop. With a sigh, he grabbed the cowboy by the legs and hurried out.

Dangling upside down, Woody clutched his

stomach as Andy stamped down the stairs. But he wasn't going to complain about a rough ride. At least he was with Andy.

Andy jumped down the front steps, then crossed to the driveway. As he passed the neatly trimmed bushes that lined the front of his house, a small plastic face poked out from between some branches.

It was Buzz Lightyear. And his temper was raging like a solar storm.

But Andy didn't see him. "I couldn't find my Buzz," Andy complained as he climbed into the van. "I know I left him right there, on my desk!"

Mrs Davis buckled Molly into her car seat, then hopped up behind the steering wheel. "Honey, I'm sure he's around. You'll find him." She started the engine.

Buzz Lightyear's helmet protected him from the exhaust fumes as he ran towards the van. At the last moment he leaped with all his strength—and grabbed on to the rear bumper just as the van pulled away. *Just you wait, cowboy!*

CHAPTER 9

"Hey, Mum. Can I help to fill the car with petrol?" Andy leaned forward in his seat and smiled at his mum. They had just pulled into a petrol station.

"Of course," Mrs Davis said. "I'll even let you drive."

"Yeah?!" Andy asked, amazed.

"Of course—when you're sixteen!"

"Yuk, yuk, yuk. Very funny, Mum."

Grinning, Mrs Davis stepped down from the van. Andy slid open the side door and hopped out to help his mum.

Lying on the back seat, Woody was miserable. His life was a complete mess. Of course, he got to come along with Andy tonight. But what joy was there in that? Now he knew there was something even more painful than being left behind:

When your body wished you were someone else.

Even worse, Woody's friends—the toys in Andy's

room—who had once admired him, now hated his guts. "How am I ever going to convince them it was an accident?" Sadly he gazed up through the open sun roof at the first stars of evening, twinkling like fireflies.

Suddenly something else from space appeared in the small square. A spaceman scowling angrily through his glass helmet.

"Buzz!"

Lightyear leapt down onto the back seat. He was covered in mud. Bits of leaves and twigs stuck to his spacesuit. And he looked furious!

But Woody was too overjoyed to notice. Buzz was here. He was okay! Oh, this was wonderful! A miracle! Woody thanked his lucky stars. Now everything was going to be all right.

"Buzz! Hah! You're alive! This is great. Oh, I'm saved. I'm saved! Andy will find you here, he'll take us back to the room, then you can explain to everybody what really happened. Right?"

Buzz didn't say a word. He just glared.

"Right . . . buddy?" Woody repeated nervously.

"I just want you to know," Buzz said calmly, "that even though you tried to terminate me, revenge is not an idea we promote on my planet."

Woody wiped a sleeve across his brow. "Whew! That's good."

"But we're not on my planet—are we?"

Before Woody could answer, Buddy lunged at the sheriff's throat. Wrestling and scuffling, they rolled off the seat, bounced onto the floor mats, then tumbled through the open door of the van.

The tarmac was hard and rough, and gas fumes filled Woody's nostrils as he and Buzz rolled beneath the vehicle, locked in mortal combat.

Buzz landed a punch that sent Woody's head spinning round on his body.

Woody countered by pummelling the spaceman's chest with both fists. The controls beeped and flashed. Buzz's helmet *whooshed* open and closed.

SLAM!

Woody and Buzz froze.

Andy and his mum had jumped back into the van and slammed the doors.

Through the open driver's-side window they could hear Mrs Davis say cheerily, "Next stop—"

"Pizza Planet!" Andy finished for her. "Yeah!"

The engine roared to life.

Then the van pulled away, its huge tyres just inches away from flattening Buzz and Woody into the tarmac. Lying in the open in a tangle of arms and legs, the two toys watched helplessly as the van's red tailights disappeared into the night.

CHAPTER 10

"Andy!" Woody couldn't believe he'd been left behind. Desperately he ran after the van. But then he stopped, panting. He was pretty fast in the toy world, but his six-inch legs could never catch up with a human-sized van.

"Doesn't he realize that I'm not there?" Woody felt as if he'd been trampled by a herd of buffalo. "I'm lost . . . I'm a lost toy!"

Behind him, Buzz flipped open his wrist communicator. "Buzz Lightyear Mission Log. The local sheriff and I seem to be at a huge refuelling station of some sort—"

"You!" Woody lunged at Buzz. It was all his fault!

But then a loud rumble shook the ground. High-beam headlights blinded them, and they froze like deer. A giant tanker!

Buzz and Woody hit the asphalt.

The tanker roared over them and stopped . . .

A millimetre from Woody's nose.

Glad to be alive, the two toys backed away from the monstrous wheels.

Buzz spoke into his wrist communicator: "According to my nava-computer—"

"Shut up!" Woody cried. "Just shut up!"

"This is no time to panic," Buzz said firmly.

"This is the *perfect* time to panic," Woody snapped. "I'm lost, Andy is gone, they're going to move away in two days—and it's *all your fault*!"

"*My* fault?" Buzz shook his head. "If you hadn't pushed me out of the window in the first place—"

"Oh, yeah? Well, if you hadn't shown up in your stupid little cardboard spaceship and taken away everything that was important to me—"

"Don't talk to me about importance," Buzz growled. "Because of you, the security of the entire universe is in jeopardy."

"What? What are you talking about?"

Buzz jammed his fists on his hips and gazed up into the starry night. He searched the constellations for a moment, then jabbed a finger towards a corner of the sky. "Right now, poised at the edge of the galaxy, Emperor Zurg has been secretly building a weapon with the destructive capacity to annihilate an entire planet. I alone have information that reveals this weapon's only weakness. And you, my friend, are responsible for delaying my rendezvous with Star Command."

Woody was speechless. This tiny toy space ranger—probably one of a million already sold—thought he was *real*. He actually believed the fate of the universe rested in his plastic hands. *Pathetic!*

Then his anger let loose, and he shook Buzz by the shoulders. "YOU ARE A TOY! Get it? You are *not* the real Buzz Lightyear. You're an action figure. You are a child's *plaything*!"

Buzz clucked his tongue. "You are a sad, strange little man and you have my pity. Farewell."

"Oh, yeah?" Woody glared at Buzz's back as he strode off into the darkness. "Well, good riddance, loony!" He walked away in the opposite direction, muttering under his breath. "Rendezvous with Star Command . . . hah!"

Ding! Ding!

Woody glanced up as a truck pulled up at the station's front door. His face lit up!

A teenager went inside to ask directions. And on the side of his truck were two of the most beautiful words Woody had ever seen: PIZZA PLANET.

It was a pizza delivery truck! All Woody had to do was get on it. Sooner or later it would head back to the restaurant where the Davis family was having dinner. With any luck, Andy and his mum would still be there!

Woody ran a few steps, then skidded to a stop. "Oh no. I can't show my face back home in Andy's room without Buzz." He scanned the car park. Buzz was at the other end, stalking away.

"Buzz!" Woody chased after him. "Come back!"

Buzz didn't even break his stride. "Go away."

"No, Buzz, you've got to come back!" Woody thought hard and fast. Any second now that delivery boy was going to drive the truck away. He and Buzz just had to be on it. Somehow he had to convince them!

He kept his eye on the truck and tried to think. Wait! That picture painted beneath the words PIZZA PLANET—it was a rocket ship! Woody snapped his fingers. "Buzz!" he shouted. "I've found a spaceship!"

Buzz spun round—and smiled.

"*Gotcha!*" Woody muttered.

Seconds later he and Buzz peeked out from behind the dirty mudflaps of the truck.

"Now, you're sure this space freighter will return to its port of origin once it jettisons its food supply?"

"Uh-huh," Woody drawled. "Then we'll be able to find a way to transport you home."

"Well, then," Buzz said firmly, "let's climb aboard." He strode towards the driver's side door.

"Wait, Buzz! Let's get in the back. No one will see us there."

"Negative," Buzz replied. "There are no restraining harnesses in the cargo area. We'll be much safer in the cockpit."

Gracefully he leapt into the air, grabbed the wing mirror, and swung himself through the open window into the cab.

Woody jumped up again and again, desperately trying to reach the mirror.

Footsteps! The driver was coming!

Panicking, Woody ran round to the rear and scrambled up over the bumper. After catching his breath, he moved forwards to peer through the window into the cab. Amazing! Buzz just sat there as if he were a VIP going for a Sunday drive with his chauffeur. Fortunately the driver couldn't see the toy, since he was hidden by a tall stack of pizzas.

Buzz dutifully hooked his seat belt, then settled back for the trip.

Woody shook his head. "Safer in the cockpit than the cargo bay," he said. "What an idiot."

The teenage driver put his foot down, screeching off into traffic. Woody, without a seat belt, slammed against the back doors and fell into a crumpled pile. He looked up just in time to see a huge black tool box tumbling towards him.

BAM!

Everything went black.

CHAPTER 11

After hurtling through the dark night for what seemed like hours, the pizza delivery truck finally screeched to a halt. Buzz waited till the driver went inside. Then he scanned the terrain.

This was Pizza Planet, all right. A sign over the door said: LAUNCH PAD ARCADE.

Beneath the sign two armoured sentries stood guard. Buzz didn't realize they were just animatronic robots. He thought they were real.

As two humans approached, the guards parted their spears. "*You-are-clear-to-enter*," the robots' recorded voices droned. "*Welcome-to-Pizza-Planet*."

Buzz turned round and pried open the sliding window. The back of the truck was empty, except for a large toolbox shoved up against the back doors. "Sheriff!" Buzz hissed.

A groggy Woody crawled out from behind the toolbox.

"Listen," Buzz said. "The entrance is heavily guarded. We need a way to get in. Got any ideas?"

Woody thought he could probably think of something . . . as soon as his head stopped pounding like a bronco trying to break out of its stall.

A few minutes later the robot guards once again parted for a human and her two children.

At the same time a burger box and a paper cup popped out of a nearby rubbish bin.

"Now!" cried the cup.

Hidden in the fast-food rubbish, Buzz and Woody rushed to the door. "Quickly, Sheriff. The airlock is closing."

Once inside, they sneaked in between some video games and threw off their disguises.

"My stars!" Buzz blinked in amazement. A carnival of sights and sounds filled the room. Pinball machines and video games pinged and flashed.

Woody scanned the mob of kids, looking for one special face. Then he saw him. Andy! He was playing a game called Black Hole while his mum watched and baby Molly slept peacefully in her pushchair.

All we have to do, Woody reasoned, *is get into that pushchair–and we're home free. Easy! Like taking candy from a baby!* He began to inch his way forwards, motioning for Buzz to follow.

But Buzz was forging his own path. "All we need is to find a ship that's heading for sector twelve."

Woody grabbed Buzz by the arm. "Uh-uh, Buzz. This way. There's a special ship."

"You mean it was hyperdrive?"

"Hyper*active*, hyperdrive," Woody assured him. "With AstroTurf. Come on." Woody darted towards Molly's pushchair, with Buzz right behind him.

Except Buzz *wasn't* right behind him. He'd stopped to stare in wonder at the most beautiful spaceship in the entire universe.

At least, that's what Buzz thought it was. It was actually a prize machine called Crane Game. The kind where a kid could drop in some money, then manipulate the steam-shovel-like claw inside to grab a prize and drop it into a slot.

This one was designed to *look* like a spaceship, though. Attached to one side stood a silvery metal frame, like a gantry used to launch a rocket. Every few seconds the machine flashed. Steam spewed out the bottom as if it were about to blast off. The recorded sounds of a rocket engine roared.

Buzz whistled and headed towards the ship.

Woody was all ready to slip into Molly's pushchair when he realized Buzz wasn't with him. He groaned. *Now, where on earth—*

Uh-oh! Buzz was scaling the gantry to the Crane Game! "Ooh! This cannot be happening to me!"

Above: Woody tries to prove that Buzz is safe with him.

Below: Buzz attempts to rescue Woody.

Above: "Listen, Lightsnack, you stay away from Andy," says Woody

Below: "How dare you open a spaceman's helmet on an uncharted planet!"

Above: "Hey, Etch! Draw!" challenges Woody.

Below: Buzz demonstrates his ability to fly, much to Woody's dismay.

Above: Babyface Spider and the other mutant toys gather round to listen to Woody's plan.

Below: The mutant toys teach Sid a lesson!

Above: Buzz and Woody are too late to catch the family car - again!

Below: Buzz and Woody race to get back to Andy.

Above: Woody is the leader of the toys, and Andy's favourite since nursery school.

Below: Buzz Lightyear is the new guy in town and could replace Woody as the favourite toy.

Above: Woody mocks Buzz Lightyear. "Buzz! L-look! An alien!"

Below: This time Woody goes too far.

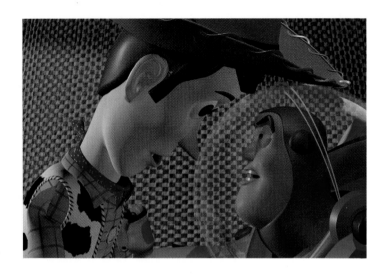

Above: Woody and Buzz fight for favourite toy status.

Below: Buzz and Woody watch as Andy's car drives out of the petrol station.

Woody mumbled as he stamped down the aisle to get him.

By the time he caught up, Buzz had managed to slip inside the machine. Woody grabbed his hat and groaned as Buzz Lightyear, airhead space ranger, leapt into a pile of squeeze-toy "aliens".

"A stranger!" one shouted. "From the outside!"

The creatures murmured and squirmed, making the mound of toys undulate like the ocean.

"Greeings! I am Buzz Lightyear! I come in peace."

"Tell us," one of the aliens begged. "What is it like outside?"

Reluctantly Woody climbed the machine. *I must have mush for brains*, he thought as he slid inside.

He plopped down into the squeaky pile of aliens just in time to hear Buzz say, "This is an intergalactic emergency. I need to commandeer your vessel to sector twelve! Who's in charge here?"

The aliens pointed upwards. A mechanical claw dangled idly above them.

"The claw!" they murmured.

"The claw is our master!" one alien cried.

"The claw chooses who will go and who will stay!" another alien crooned.

"Oh, brother!" Woody rolled his eyes. These squeeze toys were crazier than Buzz. And he had to step on them to get to the spaceman. Yuck!

But the Crane Game suddenly shook as if someone

were pounding on the side. Laughter echoed off the clear walls and ceiling.

Woody darted a glance to the front of the machine. A boy's face was pressed against the glass. It was a face from his darkest nightmares. A face from next door.

Sid Phillips.

"Look!" cried one of the aliens. "Someone summons the claw!"

"Get down!" Woody shouted. He tackled Buzz, dragging them both below a layer of aliens.

"Sheriff!" Buzz exclaimed. "What's got into you?"

But Woody just raised a finger to his lips and pointed.

Sid was stuffing money into the coin slot. The machine began to hum. Sid yanked on the joystick. Slowly the crane jerked round.

"The claw!" cried an alien. "It moves!"

Woody inched downwards as the crane hovered directly above them. The jaws of the claw snapped open, then plunged into the pile.

Woody closed his eyes. Was this how it all ended? As a cheap arcade prize for Sid Phillips?

He felt the alien just above them rise.

"Gotcha!" Sid cried.

"I have been chosen!" the little rubber creature cried joyfully. "Farewell, my friends. I go on to a better place."

But now Buzz Lightyear lay exposed at the top of the pile of aliens. Before Woody could yank him further down, Sid spotted the toy spaceman. The boy couldn't believe his eyes. Usually these machines were crammed full of cheap toys. "A Buzz Lightyear? No way!"

Sid jammed more money in for another try. The crane cranked up. Sid jerked on the joystick, steering the claw towards Buzz.

Woody searched for a way out. At the back of the machine he spotted a trap door. *Probably where they load the toys*, Woody mused. He tried to open it, but it wouldn't budge. Gathering all his strength, he slammed his shoulder against the door—and it banged open. Woody almost tumbled out, but he grabbed the edge of the hatch.

Woody leapt for Buzz, seizing him by the boots—just as the claw clamped down on his helmet.

"Yes!" Sid cried.

Woody pulled back on Buzz. But then some of the aliens began to push the spaceman upwards.

"Hey!" Woody cried. "What are you guys doing?"

"He has been chosen!" a cuddly alien explained.

"Do not fight the claw!" another warned.

Woody hung on to Buzz's leg as he felt himself dragged into the air.

"All right!" Sid cried at the sight of Buzz *and* Woody. "Double prizes!" Skillfully he manoeuvered

63

the claw towards the corner prize slot. He jabbed a red button, and the jaws flexed open.

Woody and Buzz tumbled down a long dark tunnel, then out into the light—and into the hot, grimy hands of an eager Sid Phillips.

"This is Pilot 109 Sid," he said. "The rescue mission was a success. We're going home!" Clutching his prizes, Sid hurried towards the exit.

Woody caught a glimpse of Andy across the noisy room. He was smiling in the glow of the Black Hole.

Woody wondered if it was the last time he would ever see Andy's face.

CHAPTER 12

Something shook in the bushes.

A flashlight beamed down from Andy's window. "Hey!" Rex whispered. "I think I've found him!"

"Meowwww!" A cat darted out of the shadows.

"Whiskers!" Rex called down. "Get out of here! You're interfering with our search and rescue!"

Rex ducked as headlights swept across the driveway. The Davises were home.

Bo Peep, Mr Potato Head, and the other toys clustered at the window. They watched as Mrs Davis hopped out to unbuckle Molly from her car seat. But something was wrong with Andy. He seemed upset. That was odd. He usually came home from Pizza Planet in a cheery mood.

Andy looked under the back seat. He searched the front seats, too. "Mum! Have you seen Woody?"

"Where was the last place you left him?"

"Right here in the van."

"Well, then," Mrs Davis said, walking up the front steps, "you're just not looking hard enough."

"He's not here, Mum. Woody's gone!"

Upstairs the toys looked at one another.

"Woody's gone?" Bo Peep gasped.

"That weasel!" Hamm cried. "He ran away!"

"I told you he was guilty," Mr Potato Head bragged.

One by one the toys moved away from the window.

Little Bo Peep remained a moment longer, staring out into the dark night. "*Oh, Woody,*" she murmured. But at last even she turned away, shaking her head in utter disappointment.

So none of them saw Sid Phillips ride up next door on his bike. They didn't see Woody and Buzz peek out of his back pack.

Sid stopped at his rusty, dented letter box and looked inside.

"Sheriff," Buzz whispered. "I can see your dwellings from here. You're almost home."

The squeaky alien wriggled up between them. "Nirvana is coming! The mystic portal awaits!"

"You guys just don't get it, do you?" Woody muttered. "If we go inside Sid's house, we *won't* be coming out."

Sid slammed the letter box shut, then rode up into the yard and jumped off his bike, sending it crashing to the ground. He dragged his backpack along the

66

unmown grass as he ran up to a front door that desperately needed a fresh coat of paint.

"Oh no!" Woody choked out. "We're going in!"

The toys could hear scratching and howling inside. When Sid opened the door, his smelly dog Scud ran out. The dog pounced at the backpack, but Sid scooped it up and held it high above his head.

"Sit, Scud, sit!"

The dog growled, but at last he plopped down on his rear end, drooling through sharp, wicked teeth.

"Good dog. Here, boy, I've got something for you."

Woody pressed himself down into the pack as Sid's big grimy hand plunged inside. *Squeak!* The alien toy was smiling as Sid yanked it out. But then Woody and Buzz heard it squeal.

"Here, Scud. Catch!"

It was horrifying to think they might be next!

Sid shoved open the front door and, without wiping his feet, stamped inside. "Hey, Hannah!"

Sid's stringy-haired little sister stood in the front hall holding a worn-looking Janie doll.

"Did I get my package in the post?" Sid asked.

"I dunno."

"What do you mean, you don't know?"

"I don't know!"

Sid's eyes narrowed. "Oh no!" He snatched the

doll from her hands. "Janie's so sick. I'll have to perform one of my emergency operations on her!"

"No!" Hannah cried. "Don't touch her!"

Sid ran upstairs to his room and slammed the door. He threw his backpack on the bed. Woody and Buzz peeped out again.

Woody was stunned. Sid's room was nothing like Andy's. This musty-smelling place was a total mess. The bed was unmade. Dirty clothes, mouldy snack plates, and other peculiar junk littered the floor. Shadows lurked in every corner.

Woody nudged Buzz and pointed across the room. They watched in horror as Sid tightened the Janie doll into a vice . . . then ripped her head off!

"Hannah!" Sid called. He went to the door and flung it open. His sister stood there sniffling.

Sid smiled as sweetly as a boy on a greeting card commercial. "Janie's all better now."

Hannah smiled hopefully through her tears.

Sid held up the doll.

Hannah shrieked. Janie's head was gone, and in its place—the head of a plastic pterodactyl! "Mum!" Hannah screamed as she turned and ran.

Sid tossed the doll over his shoulder and chased his sister down the hall. "She's lying, Mum! Whatever she says, it's not true, I—" The slamming door cut off the rest of his excuses.

Buzz crawled out of Sid's pack to check on the doll. Its body lay twisted on the dirty floor.

"We're going to die," Woody moaned.

Buzz turned to Woody. "Listen, Sheriff—"

But Woody was staring at the door. He wriggled out of the backpack, ran across the bed, and dived onto the doorknob.

But Sid had locked it from the outside. Woody dropped to the floor. "There's got to be another way out." A small crash made him turn.

A plastic yo-yo rolled quietly across the floor, then fell on its side.

A shadow floated past him. He whirled round.

"Buzz? . . ." Was that you?"

Two eyes blinked at him from beneath the bed, then crept toward him . . . closer and closer. Woody gulped and stepped back.

A face inched into the light, and Woody sighed in relief. It was only the head of a baby doll! It was probably shy. "Hey, hi there, little fella. Come on out. Do you know a way out of here?"

The head moved forwards out of the shadows.

Woody choked down a scream. The doll head was mounted on a spiderbike body made from the parts of an erector set. With a soft whirring sound, the babyfaced spiderlike creature stretched its metal legs till it towered over the astonished cowboy.

Woody glanced nervously around the room. Other

strange mutant toys darted out from the shadows. Toys that no toy company had ever imagined, that no child had ever wished for. At least, no normal child.

Woody clambered back up on the bed and cowered behind Buzz. They watched as Babyface Spider dragged the mutant Janie doll into the shadows. Another mutant toy snatched up the doll's head. Two other toys picked at the pterodactyl body Sid had left in the vise. At last they pulled it free.

Woody's guts lurched. "They're cannibals!"

He leaped into the backpack, with Buzz right behind him. Quickly they zipped it shut.

Buzz punched a button on his chest. "Mayday! Come in, Star Command. Send reinforcements!" He paused. "Star Command, do you copy?"

No response. Buzz sighed.

"Sheriff," he said. "Until Star Command shows up, we'll just have to hold off these creatures ourselves." He adjusted a knob on his suit. *Blip!* "I've just set my laser from stun to kill."

"Great," Woody muttered. "If those creatures attack, you can just blink 'em to death."

CHAPTER 13

ater, Sid was playing with Buzz and Woody. "Mission control. The pilot is ready for testing."

Buzz Lightyear cringed as Sid pulled the trigger on an electric drill. He'd just been strapped to the bit.

"He's pulling some good g-forces now!" Sid switched to a higher speed. Buzz wobbled violently.

"Mayday!" Sid shouted. "He's breaking up!"

Buzz flew off the drill and smashed against the dartboard before crumpling to the ground.

Then Sid's gaze fell on Woody. "A survivor!" He snatched him up. "Where is the real base? Talk!"

He pulled Woody's string and got a prerecorded answer: "*I'd like to join your posse, boys, but first I'm going to sing a little song.*"

"Liar!" Sid shouted and dropped him to the floor. "We have ways of making you talk . . ."

Sid opened the blinds. Early-afternoon sunlight

slanted sharply through the windowpane. He held up a magnifying glass and slowly, carefully, directed a concentrated beam of sunlight on to Woody's face. After only a few moments a tiny wisp of smoke curled up from the toy's forehead.

"Where are your rebel friends now?" Sid smirked.

"Si-iiid!" his mother shouted from downstairs. "Your fish fingers are ready!"

"All right!" Sid hollered back. He threw down the magnifying glass and ran out of the room.

As soon as he was gone, Woody let out a howl. Fanning his face, he dashed towards a nearby bowl of half-eaten cereal and dunked his whole head into the tepid milk. "Ahhhhhh."

Buzz ran over and pulled Woody out, searching his face for damage. Then he grinned and whacked Woody on the back. "I'm proud of you, Sheriff. A lesser man would have talked under such torture."

Woody sighed and looked at his reflection in the rounded side of the cereal spoon. He rubbed at a black smudge. "I really hope this isn't permanent."

Then he noticed something else reflected in the spoon and grabbed Buzz's arm. "The door! Sid left it open! We're free!"

"But Woody, we don't know what's out there!"

Suddenly Babyface crawled into Woody's path, followed by several other mutilated toys.

"They're gonna eat us, Buzz. Do something!"

"Shield your eyes!" Buzz cried. He fired his laser at the mutants. *Beep! Beep!*

Nothing happened.

"Hey, it's not working. Darn! I'm sure I recharged it before I left. It should be good—"

"You idiot!" Woody shrieked. "You're a toy! Use your karate action!" He pushed a button on Buzz's spacesuit. The spaceman's arm chopped up and down.

"Hey, what are you doing?" Buzz cried. "Stop!"

But Woody ignored him. He held Buzz in front of him and backed towards the door as the arm chopped up and down. "Get back!" he shouted at the mutants.

The toys retreated into the shadows.

"Sorry, guys," Woody said when he reached the door, "but dinner's cancelled." He let go to Buzz and ran. "There's no place like home . . . there's no place like home . . ." he murmured as he flew down the unpolished hallway.

But he stopped at the top of the stairs. Scud the dog was sprawled across the first step, snoring loudly. Woody backed up. Then someone grabbed him and pulled him back down the hall.

"Another stunt like that, cowboy, and you're going to get us both killed."

"Hey, Buzz, don't tell me what to do—"

"Shhhhhh!"

Buzz motioned for Woody to follow him. They

crawled on hands and knees along the floor. Woody didn't notice that the ring on his pullstring got caught on the railing. With each inch he crawled, he pulled the string tighter and tighter.

Snap! The ring slipped loose. One of Woody's pre-recorded messages echoed down the canyons of the hallway: "*YEEEEEEEE-HAAAAAAAAAA ...*"

Buzz and Woody jumped in surprise.

Scud woke up, growling before he'd even opened one eye.

"*Giddyup, pardner!*" Woody's voice box talked on.

Scud bounded up the stairs.

"Split up!" Buzz ordered as he dived through an open doorway on the left.

Woody flung himself through the door on the right. It was a junk-stuffed cupboard. As he slammed the door behind him, an unsteady tower of clutter crashed to the floor.

Scud prowled back and forth, growling and sniffing through the crack beneath the door. Across the hall Buzz watched nervously to see what Scud would do.

Scud turned and was poised to enter the TV room where Buzz was hiding. Suddenly Mr Phillips, who lay dozing in front of the television, let out a loud snore. The dog hesitated and tentatively began to enter the room. But another snore sent Scud scuttling downstairs again with his tail between his legs. Buzz breathed a sigh of relief. He tiptoed into the hall. . . .

"Calling Buzz Lightyear! Come in, Buzz Lightyear! This is Star Command!"

Buzz whirled round. There, in front of Mr Phillips, was a TV screen filled with an image of outer space. A man's deep voice beckoned: *"Buzz Lightyear! Do you read me?"*

"Star Command!" Buzz cried. Quickly he flipped open his wrist communicator. He started to speak, then heard a child answer for him:

"Buzz Lightyear responding! I read you loud and clear!"

Buzz stared at the television screen. The image of outer space faded into a pleasant view of an ordinary back yard, where two kids played happily . . . with Buzz Lightyear toys.

"Planet Earth needs your help!"

One of the kids spoke into a plastic wrist communicator: *"Buzz Lightyear is on his way!"*

Totally confused, Buzz stepped closer.

A second kid flew a boxed Buzz Lightyear action figure through the air and landed him in the grass. The box looked like the spaceship Buzz had left behind in Andy's room!

"Yes, kids," the announcer said, *"Buzz Lightyear, the world's greatest superhero is now the world's greatest toy!"*

75

Buzz winced at the word *toy* as if he'd been struck. He tried to turn away. But the horrible images were impossible for him to ignore. The figure on the screen looked so much like him, it could have been his twin.

As the announcer's voice droned on, ordinary kids demonstrated each new feature described. *"Every Buzz Lightyear comes with a locking wrist communicator. Real-life karate action. Pulsating laserlight. And multiphrase voice simulator."* One by one, Buzz compared the features on the screen to himself.

Buzz choked as he heard the TV toy say, *"It's a secret mission in uncharted space! Let's go."*

Buzz pushed the button on the chest of his spacesuit and heard: *"It's a secret mission in unchanted space! Let's go."* The same message—in exactly the same voice!

"Best of all," the announcer added, *"activate Buzz Lightyear's high-pressure space wings."*

The Buzz Lightyear toy on television seemed to fly majestically across an uncharted planet. The Buzz voice cried, *"To infinity and beyond!"* Then the picture froze and a disclaimer flashed across the screen: NOT A FLYING TOY.

"Not a flying toy," the announcer repeated quickly. *"So get your Buzz Lightyear action figure today—and save a galaxy near you!"*

A local announcer's voice added: *"Available at all Al's Toy Barn outlets."*

76

His mind reeling, Buzz staggered towards the door. He glanced at his wrist communicator and saw something he'd never noticed before. Tiny lettering was pressed into the plastic: MADE IN TAIWAN.

Buzz stared heavenwards. A small stained glass window was partly open. In the distance a bird soared gracefully across the sky.

Woody's taunting words echoed now in Buzz's mind: "*You are a toy! You can't fly!*"

Suddenly Buzz stood up straight and tall. His eyes sparkled with determination. This was all some kind of weird mistake. He'd show them he could fly. He'd show them all!

He climbed up on the banister, then pressed the button that released his magnificent "high-pressure space wings." Smiling and determined, he aimed himself towards the stained glass window . . . and that little patch of blue sky.

"To infinity and beyond!"

Buzz leapt off the banister.

And fell like a pound of nails . . . down, down, to the hard floor below. CRUNCH!

For a few moments he didn't move. Then Buzz moaned and rolled over. Slowly he opened his eyes.

His visor was cracked. And his right arm was completely broken off at the shoulder. At first he stared at it, shocked. But then he simply turned away and lay still.

What did it matter anyway? he told himself. *After all, he was only a toy.*

He lay there, miserable and didn't even care when Sid's kid sister, Hannah, picked him up and took him to her room.

CHAPTER 14

Tangled in dusty Christmas lights, Woody crawled through the mountains of rubbish and out into the hall.

"Hey, Buzz?" he called out softly. "Where are you? The coast is clear."

Buzz's voice bellowed from down the hall. "*It's a secret mission in uncharted space. Let's go!*"

"Really?" Woody heard Sid's sister Hannah coo. "That is soooo interesting."

Woody crept towards the voices till he reached an open doorway. Hannah's bedroom, Woody thought. Cautiously he peeked inside.

Buzz was in there, all right. Suffering outrageous humiliation at the hands of Sid's kid sister!

Hannah was having a tea party. Seated around a tiny table were several headless dolls. Buzz Lightyear was propped up at the head of the table, dressed in a frilly apron and adorable party hat.

"It's so nice of you to join us, Mrs Nesbit,"

Hannah said to Buzz. She used his severed arm to pour the tea. "What a lovely hat! It goes quite well with your head."

Woody thought hard and fast. He had to put a stop to this! But what could he do?

Then he snapped his fingers. *Got it!* he thought.

Yanking off his cowboy hat, he ran down the hall to the top of the stairs. He cleared his throat, then spoke into his hat to help disguise his voice. He tried to make his voice sound high and feminine—like Mrs Phillips's—as he called out loudly: "Hannah! Oh, Hannah!"

Hannah stopped pouring tea and looked up. "Mum?" She turned back to her dolls. "Please excuse me, ladies. I'll be right back."

In response, Buzz keeled over and landed—*splash!*—face down in his teacup. Hannah hurried out of the room—right past Woody, who lay still under the tangled string of Christmas lights. "What is it, Mum? Mum—where are you?"

As soon as Hannah disappeared down the stairs, Woody sprang to life and bolted into her bedroom.

"Buzz! Are you okay?" He picked up Buzz's broken-off arm. "What happened to you?"

Buzz bolted upright, with a glazed look in his eye. "One minute you're defending the whole galaxy—" he grabbed his arm from Woody and pointed it at the headless dolls—"then suddenly you find yourself drinking tea with Marie Antoinette and her little sisters!"

The headless dolls turned and waved.

Woody choked back a feeling of disgust and helped Buzz to his feet. "I think you've had enough tea for today, pal. Let's get you out of here."

Suddenly Buzz grabbed Woody by the collar. "Don't you get it?" he shrieked, laughing hysterically. "You see this hat?" I am Mrs Nesbit!"

Woody shook the spaced-out spaceman by the shoulders. "Snap out of it, Buzz!" He pressed the button to pop open Buzz's helmet. He slapped him just enough to startle him. Then he politely closed the helmet.

Buzz seemed to regain his composure then. He shook his head as he and Woody walked out into the hall. "I'm sorry," he said with a sigh. "You're right. I suppose I'm just a little depressed, that's all—"

Suddenly Buzz dropped to his knees on the hardwood floor. "Oh, I'm a sham!" he wailed.

"Shhhhh!" Woody hissed nervously. "Quiet, Buzz!"

"Look at me," Buzz ranted on. "I can't even fly through a window. But—the hat looks good, right? Tell me the hat looks good . . ."

Woody stopped. He fingered the string of Christmas lights still wrapped round him. "Through the window . . ." he mumbled, thinking.

The law man peeped down the hall. The door to Sid's room was open. And one window in his room faced Andy's house!

"Buzz, you're a genius!" he cried. He grabbed his fellow prisoner and dragged him towards Sid's room. "Come on, come on—this way!"

Buzz stumbled after him, moaning. "Years of Academy training . . . wasted!"

Hamm and Mr Potato Head were playing the game Battleship. Hamm was winning. He'd already won Mr Potato Head's hat and nose. Now he was going for his moustache. Or maybe his big mouth. Mr Potato Head's bad mood was getting worse. He hated to lose face!

Not much else was going on in Andy's room. Bo Peep was daydreaming, barely tending her sheep. Rex was practicing scary faces. Slinky was curled up, snoozing in a patch of sun. Things just hadn't been the same since Buzz disappeared and Woody ran off.

No one noticed at first that someone was waving to them from the house next door.

That someone finally managed to pry open. Sid's window "Hey, guys! Guys! Over here!"

Mr Potato Head got up and wobbled towards the window. "Son of a building block! It's Woody!"

Hamm stared in astonishment. "He's in Sid the psycho's bedroom."

"Woody?" Bo Peep said.

"You're kidding!" Rex said.

As they flocked to the window, Woody waved like crazy. "Ho, boy. Am I glad to see you guys!"

"I knew you'd come back!" Slinky cried loyally.

"What are you doing over *there?*" Bo Peep asked.

"It's a long story," Woody said. "I'll explain later." He held out the string of Christmas lights. "Here! Catch!" With the skill of a cowpuncher used to roping cattle, Woody tossed the string of lights towards Andy's window. Slinky grabbed the end.

"Great going, Slink!" Woody called. "Now, just tie it onto something."

"Wait!" Mr Potato Head grabbed the lights. "I've got a better idea. How about we *don't*!"

"Hey!" Slinky said.

"Mr Potato Head!" Bo Peep cried.

"Did you all take stupid pills this morning? Have you forgotten what he did to Buzz?" He shook his head in astonishment. "And now you want to let him back over here?"

Woody was stunned. Of course, Mr Potato Head had always been a little rough, a little sarcastic. But that was just his nature. He couldn't believe the toy would completely turn against him. "You've got it all wrong, Potato Head. Buzz is fine! He's right here with me!"

"You are a liar!" Mr Potato Head shot back.

"No, I'm not." Woody turned back to Sid's room.

"Hey, Buzz, come here and tell me all the nice toys that you're not dead."

But Buzz Lightyear didn't even seem to hear. He just sat on the floor, staring at his broken-off arm. With a disgusted sigh, he peeled the sticker off his wrist communicator, then crumpled it and tossed it to the floor like a used sweet wrapper.

Woody groaned. "Uh, just a sec," he called over to his old friends. "Come on, Buzz," he hissed. "Will you please get up here and give me a hand!"

Buzz tossed him his broken arm with the hand still attached.

"Ha, ha, very funny." Woody glared at the toy, then exploded: "Come on, Buzz, this is serious!"

"Woooody!" Slinky hollered. "Where'd you go?"

"He's lying," Mr Potato Head told the crowd. "Buzz isn't there."

Woody rushed back to the window. The crowd was getting rowdy. *Only one thing to do*, Woody told himself. *Better give 'em a good show*.

"Oh, hi, Buzz," he said, trying to act casual. "Why don't you say hello to the guys next door?"

Woody held up Buzz's severed arm and waved it in front of the window, careful not to let the broken end show to his friends. Turning his face away, he did his best Buzz Lightyear impression: "Hi ya, fellas. To infinity and beyond."

"Hey, look!" Rex said. "It's Buzz!"

Bo Peep clapped her hands. "He's okay!"

Whew! They're buying it! Woody thought in relief. "Uh, hey, Buzz. Let's show 'em our new secret bestfriends handshake!" He shook Buzz's hand. The arm bent down at an awkward angle.

Mr Potato Head's eyes narrowed.

Hamm squinted. "Something's screwy here . . ."

"So you see?" Woody went on. "We're friends now, guys. Aren't we, Buzz?"

"You bet! Give me a hug!"

"Oh, sure," Woody answered himself. "I love you, too."

Slinky had seen enough. "See? It *is* Buzz. Now give me back the lights, Potato Head."

But Mr Potato Head just shoved the Slinky dog aside. "Wait just a minute," he said suspiciously. "Hey!" he shouted at Woody. "What are you trying to pull?"

Nervously Woody raised both hands in the air and shrugged. "Nothing!"

Mr Potato Head gasped.

Rex was nearly sick.

Bo Peep screamed and buried her face in her hands.

But Slinky couldn't tear his eyes away from the lawman he had once admired.

Woody was holding Buzz's severed arm in the air.

"That is *disgusting*!" Hamm said.

"Murderer!" Mr Potato Head cried.

Too late, Woody realized his mistake. "No, no! It's not what you think. I swear!"

"Save it for the jury!" Mr Potato Head snapped. "I hope Sid pulls your voice box out, ya creep!" He flung the string of Christmas lights out of the window. It banged against the side of Sid's house, tinkling as a few bulbs smashed.

"Don't leave!" Woody cried desperately. "You've got to help us, please. You don't know what it's like over here!"

A cold winter wind seemed to grip his heart as he read the betrayal in his friends' eyes. One by one they drifted away from the window. Only Slinky—good old faithful Slinky—still remained.

"Slink! Please listen to me!" Woody begged.

But Slinky the dog could no longer look the cowboy in the eye. With a whimper, he lowered the blinds.

"No!" Desperate, Woody screamed, "Come back. SLI-I-I-I-INKYYY!"

His voice was drowned out by the first rumblings of a thunderstorm.

CHAPTER 15

Woody stood alone at the window, watching Andy's house. He was close enough to sail a paper aeroplane through Andy's window. But it might as well have been a million miles away for all the chance he had of getting home again.

Depressed, Woody gloomily considered ripping Buzz's other arm off. But then he heard a noise on the floor.

The mutant toys were attacking Buzz! Woody watched in horror as Babyface grabbed the spaceman's broken-off arm.

Quickly the lawman rushed to the rescue.

"Aaaaahhhh!" he shouted, ready to fight. "All right, you cannibals. Get back!"

He grabbed at the arm Babyface held in his mouth.

One last yank sent Woody flying across the room. He crashed into the wall. Shaking his head, he realized his hands were empty. The mutants still had Buzz's arm.

His stomach lurched as he watched the mutants swarm over Buzz's lifeless body. He wasn't even fighting back! "Hey!" Woody shouted. "He's still alive. And you're not gonna get him, you monsters!"

Woody fought wildly. He grabbed at the repulsive toys, tossing creatures left and right, trying to get to Buzz.

When he finally reached the centre of the mob, the mutant toys unexpectedly melted back into the shadows.

Woody had expected to find a half-mutilated spaceman toy. Instead, Buzz Lightyear sat up with a puzzled look on his face, rubbing his re-attached arm.

Confused, Woody reached out and touched the arm, the hand. Yep, good as new. "Hey, they fixed you! Why would they do that?"

Gazing round the room, Woody saw that the Janie doll and the pterodactyl had been repaired, too.

He turned towards the mutants, but they scurried back, as if afraid he might attack them again. *What's going on?* Woody wondered.

But there was no time to find out. Sid was back. Right outside the door!

Woody grabbed Buzz and tried to drag him to safety. "Come on, Buzz. Get up." But Buzz jerked his arm away and continued to stare at the floor.

"Fine!" Woody grunted. "Let Sid trash you. But don't blame me."

Buzz was lying in the middle of the floor when the door swung open.

Woody hid under a plastic milk crate, the kind used for storing toys. He slipped beneath it just as Sid rushed in, carrying a package.

"It came!" he crowed. "It finally came!" His voice dropped to a reverent whisper. "The big one!"

He ripped open the package. Inside lay a rocket with the words THE BIG ONE printed on its side. Sid squinted at another small sticker and read, "'Extremely dangerous. Keep out of reach of children.' *Cool* . . ."

He looked round. "Now. What am I gonna blow? Hey . . . where's that wimpy cowboy doll?"

He shoved some junk off his desk, looking for Woody. He spotted the milk crate and picked it up.

No cowboy. Sid didn't see Woody hanging on the inside. Then Sid's sights fell on Buzz Lightyear.

Sid put the milk crate down on his desk. He grabbed Buzz and picked up his tool box. He set the tool box on top of the crate and opened it up. Trapped beneath the crate, Woody heard Sid dig around in the tool box, but he couldn't see what the kid was doing.

Then Sid sniggered and stepped back.

Woody gasped. Sid had taped Buzz to the rocket!

"All right—to infinity and beyond!" Sid cackled as he grabbed some matches and started for the door.

BA-ROOM! A huge thunderclap stopped him in his tracks. Thick raindrops pelted the window-panes. "Awww . . ." But then his frown turned into a grin. "Sid Phillips reporting," he said as if he were a TV journalist. "Launch of the shuttle has been delayed due to adverse weather conditions at the launch site. Tomorrow's forecast: sunny. Ha ha ha."

He smacked Buzz down on the desk top, set his alarm clock, and placed it, ticking right next to Buzz's ear. With a sickly-sweet smile he whispered to the spaceman, "Sweet dreams . . ."

Next door Mrs Davis was tucking her son back into bed. Andy had been searching everywhere for his two missing toys. Each time he thought of a new place, he got out of bed to look.

"But what if we leave them behind?" Andy asked.

Mrs Davis smoothed Andy's hair back off his forehead. "Don't worry, honey. I'm sure we'll find Woody and Buzz before we leave tomorrow."

Andy just sighed.

Later, after Mrs Davis was gone, after Andy had fallen asleep at last, Bo Peep peeked around a moving box that said ANDY'S TOYS! KEEP OUT!

She watched Andy tossing and turning in his sleep and wondered if he was dreaming of his lost toys.

"Oh, Woody," she whispered towards the rainy window. "If only you could see how much Andy's missing you."

And she worried. Tomorrow was moving day. Would she and her friends ever see Woody or Buzz Lightyear again?

oody peeped out through the bars of his milk-crate prison. The street light gleaming through the rain-drizzled window painted eerie shadows on the sleeping face of Sid Phillips.

Across the desktop the once-proud Buzz Lightyear was still shamefully taped to the rocket. "Psst! Hey, Buzz!"

No response.

Woody picked up a few stray pennies and tossed them at Buzz, trying to get his attention.

Clink! One of the pennies struck Buzz's helmet. Slowly, listlessly, he looked over.

Woody waved wildly. "Hey! Get over here and see if you can get his tool box off of me!"

Buzz just stared.

"What?" Woody said. "What are you looking at me like that for? Hey, I didn't do anything. You're the one who wouldn't hide. It's your own fault you're strapped to that thing."

Buzz sighed and looked away.

Fuming, Woody shook the bars of the plastic milk crate like a monkey in a cage. Above him the heavy lid of the tool box slammed shut. Woody froze.

Sid rolled over in his sleep and muttered something about a pony. But he didn't wake up.

"All right," Woody whispered to Buzz. "I'm sorry. Okay? Is that what you want to hear? I shouldn't have left you out there for Sid. But you gotta admit, you weren't helping much."

Buzz responded like a toy whose battery had worn down. He didn't even move.

"Oh, come on, Buzz," Woody pleaded. "I can't do this without you. I—I need your help."

"I can't help," Buzz said flatly. "I can't help anyone."

Buzz was talking! Woody took that as a good sign. "Why, of course you can, Buzz. Come on. You can get me out of here and then I'll get that rocket off you and we'll make a break for Andy's house. Hmmmm? How 'bout it?"

"Andy's house . . . Sid's house . . ." Buzz shrugged. "What's the difference?"

"What's the difference? Whoa, Buzz, you've had a big fall. I don't think you're thinking clearly."

"No, Woody," Buzz responded. "For the first time in my life I *am* thinking clearly. You were right all along. I'm *not* a space ranger. I'm just a toy. A stupid, little insignificant toy."

"Wait a minute," Woody said indignantly. "Being a toy is a lot better than being a space ranger."

"Yeah, right."

"No, it is!" Woody insisted. He pointed out the window towards Andy's room. "Look, Buzz—over in that house is a kid who thinks you're the greatest, and it's not 'cause you're a space ranger, pal. It's because you're a *toy*. *His* toy!"

Buzz looked down at himself, at his plastic parts and fake sticker control panel. "But . . . why would Andy want *me*?"

Woody sighed and shook his head. "Why would Andy want you? Just look at you! You're Buzz Lightyear! Any other toy would give up his moving parts just to be you. You've got wings. You light up. You talk. Your helmet does that . . . that *whoosh* thing. Hey, you are one *cool* toy."

Woody couldn't tell if he'd convinced Buzz or not. But he's certainly convinced himself. His spirit drooped like a deflated party balloon.

"As a matter of fact," he went on, "you're too cool. I mean—what chance does a toy like me have against a Buzz Lightyear action figure? All I can do is . . ." Woody pulled his own string.

"*There's a snake in my boots!*" his voice box chirped. Woody shook his head in disgust. "Why would Andy ever want to play with *me* . . . when he's got *you*?" He sighed. "I'm the one who should be strapped to that rocket."

Woody glanced at the window. The rain had stopped while they were talking. A new day would be dawning soon.

Moving day. By nightfall Andy would be gone—forever.

"Listen, Buzz. Forget about me. You should get out of here while you can." He looked up.

Buzz was gone.

CHAPTER 17

Suddenly the milk crate began to shake. Woody hung on and stared up. With the rocket still taped to his back, Buzz stood on top of the crate, trying to push the tool box off.

"Buzz, what are you doing?" Woody asked. "I thought you were—"

"Woody," Buzz said, grunting. "Come on, Sheriff. There's a kid over there who needs us. Now let's get you out of this thing."

Together they struggled to free Woody.

By now the sun was rising, warm and bright, drying up the night's rain. And then they heard the sound they'd been dreading: the rumble of a moving lorry pulling into Andy's drive!

"Buzz! We've got to get out of here—now!"

Buzz pressed back against the wall and pushed against the tool box with his feet. The tool box was moving! But then it snagged against the edge of the milk crate.

CRASH! The tool box and the milk crate fell off the desk, dragging Woody with them.

Buzz glanced at Sid—miraculously the boy was still snoring away—then ran to the edge of the desk. "Woody!" he whispered. "Are you all right?"

Woody crawled out from the rubble of tools, a little wobbly and waved. He was free!

BRRIIIIIIIINNNGG!

The alarm clock rang. Sid bolted upright in his bed. With one eye half open, he felt around his desk, grabbed his hammer, and raised it to smash the clock.

Then his eye fell on Buzz. "Oh, yeah . . ." he said, remembering. He threw off the covers, then smashed the clock anyway, just for the heck of it.

Humming, Sid threw on up some clothes, grabbed Buzz and the rocket, and bolted from the room.

The second Sid was gone, Woody leapt to catch the door before it closed. He pulled it open.

"*GRRRRRRRRR!*" Scud! The dog pounced—

Woody slammed the door. A shiver ran down his spine as he listened to the dog barking and scratching on the other side, trying to get in.

"What do I do now? Come on, Woody. Think!"

Slowly, quietly, the mutant toys crept out from their hiding places, watching Woody pace the floor.

Woody snapped his fingers. "Guys!"

The toys scattered like frightened mice.

"No, wait! Listen to me!" Woody called urgently. "No, no, no, no! Wait! Wait! Listen! Please! There's a good toy down there and he's—he's going to be blown to bits in a few minutes all because of ME. We've gotta save him!" He paused and motioned with both arms for them to come closer. "I need your help."

The toys stayed hidden.

"Please. He's my friend—the only I've got."

Babyface crawled out of the corner, a smile on his face. He whistled for the others. Slowly they, too, emerged from the shadows, encircling the toy sheriff.

Woody knelt in the middle and showed the toys the ring on his pullstring. "I think I know what to do. And if it works, it will help us all."

CHAPTER 18

Woody studied his little map of the Phillipses' house. "All right, listen up. I need Pump Boy here. Ducky here. Legs?"

A toy fishing rod with fashion-doll legs strolled up.

"You're with Ducky." He jerked a thumb at a rubber ducky with a baby-doll torso and a bathroom plunger base. "RollerBob and I don't move till we get the signal. Clear?"

"Quack!"

"Okay, let's move!"

Ducky and Legs pulled the metal plate off a heating vent and disappeared inside.

Several other toys stacked up like a bizarre-looking totem pole to reach the doorknob. Woody jumped on RollerBob, a skateboard with a soldier's head and arms tied to the front. "Wind the frog!"

An army tank with a rabbit head began to wind up a little plastic frog mounted on big wheels.

Scud was still barking outside Sid's door. The toys manned their positions, eyes on Woody, whose arm was raised in the air. "Wait for the signal."

Meanwhile, Ducky and Legs had crawled through the heating ducts to the front of the house. Ducky tied the end of Legs' fishing line round his waist. They removed the porch light socket. Then Legs lowered Ducky through the opening.

Dangling in front of the front door, Ducky began to swing, back and forth, enlarging the arc. At last he swung far enough to reach his target.

The front doorbell. *Dingdong!*

Back in Sid's room, Woody sliced down with his arm. "Go!"

The totem of toys yanked open the door. The windup frog was let loose. The plastic amphibian zipped between Scud's legs and down the hallway. Barking madly, the dog chased it.

Out front, Ducky rang the bell again.

"I'll get it!" the toys heard Hannah shout. She opened the front door. No one was there.

The windup frog hurtled through the open door.

Hannah spun round when she heard Scud romping down the stairs. Ducky dropped down and nabbed Frog with his plunger. Then Legs reeled them in.

Scud burst through Hannah's legs, knocking her down as he raced onto the porch. He stopped and looked round, barking moronically, then looked up at the frog disappearing into a hole in the roof. With a growl, he realized he'd been duped. He tried to scoot back inside, but Hannah was irked. She slammed the front door. "Stupid dog."

Meanwhile, RollerBob zoomed into the kitchen with Woody and the other mutant toys clinging to his skateboard back. Bob aimed his helmeted head forwards—*bam!*—as they crashed into the back door. Woody and the other toys flew through the small square-pet-door flap. They were free!

The mutant toys found hiding places in the yard.

Woody crept round the corner of the house and parted the bushes. In the side yard he spotted Buzz, still taped to the rocket and tied to a makeshift launchpad stuck in the ground.

The cowboy scurried towards his friend.

"Woody!" Buzz whispered. "Help me out of this!"

"Shhhhh!" Woody said. "It's okay, everything's under control." He grinned confidently, then lay down on a patch of grass a few feet away.

"Woody!" Buzz squawked. "What are you doing?"

Just then Sid came out of the tool shed. Buzz and Woody froze into their action-figure postures.

"Houston, all systems are go," Sid said, pretending to be doing a real space launch. "Requesting permission to—hey!" He spotted the toy sheriff lying

101

on the ground and picked him up. "How'd you get out here?" He looked around, confused. "Oh well." He stuck a kitchen match in Woody's vest pocket and tossed him onto the barbecue grill. "You and I can have a little cookout later," he cackled madly.

"Houston, sorry for the delay. Do we have permission to launch?" Sid covered his mouth and nose with his hand to make his voice sound like a speaker: "Roger. Permission granted. You are confirmed at T minus one. Ten! Nine! Eight! . . ."

Sid struck a match and moved towards the fuse. But before he could light it, a voice rang out:

"Reach for the sky!"

Sid froze. "Huh?" He whirled round.

Woody was still lying stiffly on the grill. Sid knew he hadn't pulled the toy's string. But sound kept coming from his voice box: *"This town ain't big enough for the two of us!"*

"Wait a minute . . ." Sid said.

"Draw!" Woody snarled.

Sid picked up the toy cowboy. His voice box kept going: *"Somebody's poisoned the water hole!"*

"Man, this toy's busted."

"Who are you calling *busted*, Buster?"

Sid stopped and stared at Woody, eyes wide.

"That's right. I'm talking to *you*, Sid Phillips."

"What?" Sid shook the toy. Why was it still talking? And why was it saying such weird stuff?

"We don't like being blown up, Sid. Or smashed. Or ripped apart. . . ."

Sid was shaking. "W-w-we?"

"That's right, *we*," Woody said. "Your toys."

Woody peeped across the yard and stifled a grin. Mutant toys from Sid's bedroom and the yard rose from hiding places like creatures in a horror movie. Sid trembled with fear as the broken and mutilated toys surrounded him.

"From now on you must take good care of your toys," Woody went on. "Because if you don't, we'll find out, Sid. Because we toys—Woody's head spun around 360 degrees—"can see everything!"

As Sid stared in horror at Woody's head, the toy's rigid plastic features suddenly came to life. "So play nice," Woody warned, wagging his finger.

"AAAAAAAAAAGGGGGGGGGHHHHHH!!!!"

Sid dropped Woody as if he were on fire and bolted towards the house. At the door he bumped into Hannah. She clutched her doll protectively.

"*The toys are ALIVE!*" Sid screamed. He stared at Hannah's doll. Then he reached for it with a trembling hand. Hannah cringed. But Sid just patted it gently. "Nice dolly!" he said nervously. Then he ran upstairs and locked himself in his room.

Hannah shook her head. Brothers! She would never, ever understand them!

Sid's broken, twisted toys gathered round Woody and cheered. Woody shook the toys' hands, if they had hands, or patted them fondly on the most appropriate part.

"Nice work fellas." Woody chuckled. "Coming out of the ground. What a nice touch!"

"Woody!"

Woody turned. Buzz was still tied to the launch-pad. He held out a hand. "Thanks."

Woody grinned and shook hands with his friend.

HONK! HONK! The celebration was cut short by the sound of a moving lorry.

Through the fence that surrounded Sid's yard, they saw Mrs Davis wipe a tear from her eye. "Say goodbye to the house," she told her children.

"Goodbye, house!" Andy shouted.

"Woody!" The van!" Buzz cried.

The side door to the family van slammed shut. The Davises were leaving—for good!

Woody freed Buzz from the launchpad, but there was no time to remove the rocket taped to his back. Together the cowboy and the spaceman sprinted towards the fence. The slim cowboy easily slipped through. But Buzz got stuck because of the rocket on his back. "Woody, help me! I'm stuck!"

Woody stopped, paralyzed. Buzz was trapped in the fence. He couldn't get out by himself.

But the van was pulling away!

CHAPTER 19

Woody panicked. *I just can't leave the guy!* He tried to think clearly as he ran back to Buzz and yanked and tugged till he pulled the spaceman through the fence. Together they raced down the drive, little caring who might see them. But they stopped as they saw the Davises' van disappear down the street.

HOOOONK! The moving truck almost ran over them. As soon as it passed, Buzz began to chase it. "Come on!" he called to Woody.

Back at Sid's house, Scud was moping on the porch. But he perked up at the sight of two little action toys coming down the street.

A leather strap dangled off the back of the moving van. Buzz leapt for it . . . and caught it! Grunting, he climbed up the strap and onto the van's bumper. Then Woody lunged—but missed when the van changed gears and blew exhaust in his face.

"You can do it, Woody," Buzz called out.

Woody tried again. This time he caught hold of the strap. "I made it!"

But then he shrieked as he felt Scud's jaws chomp down on his leg. "Get away, you stupid dog! Down! Down!" His hands slipped on the chain.

"Hold on, Woody!" Buzz cried.

"I can't do it!" Woody gasped. "Take care of Andy for me . . ."

"Nooo!" Bravely Buzz leapt onto the dog's face and snapped his eyelids. The dog yelped and let go of Woody. Quickly the cowboy scrambled up the strap and unlocked the back door. When the moving lorry screeched to a halt at a red light, the door flew upwards, with Woody dangling from the handle.

But inside he spotted what he was looking for: several boxes scrawled with the words ANDY'S TOYS! KEEP OUT! Woody jumped down and yanked one open.

Mr Potato Head, Rex, and some of the other toys squinted in the sudden burst of sunlight.

"What's going on?" Rex whined.

"Woody!" Slinky cried. "How'd you get in here?"

But Woody was busy rummaging through another box. "There you are!" He pulled out the remote-control car. Then he ran to the back of the van, held up the toy car, and threw it into the street.

"What's he doing?" Bo Peep exclaimed.

"Oh, no!" Rex wailed. "He's at it again!"

Woody turned on the remote and steered the car toward Buzz. Scud had him trapped under a car parked nearby. When the toy car zoomed by him, Buzz jumped on. Woody guided the car to follow the moving truck as the red light turned green.

Scud gave chase, but Buzz headed right into the intersection and Scud couldn't follow him.

The toys in the moving box couldn't see what was going on. All they saw was Woody throwing more toys out of the back of the lorry.

"Get him!" Mr Potato Head shouted, leading a mob of angry toys out of the box.

Rocky the wrestler grabbed Woody and spun him over his head. Since Woody was still holding the remote control, the toy car did figure eights through the traffic.

"Throw him overboard!" Mr Potato Head suggested.

"No, wait!" Woody pleaded. "You don't understand. Buzz is out there! We gotta help him!"

But his friends didn't believe him. "So long, Woody!" Mr Potato Head sneered as Rocky threw Woody out.

Woody hit the ground hard. A horn blasted as a car swerved to avoid running over him.

But then Buzz scooped him up in the toy car.

"Thanks for the ride," Woody said. "Now let's catch up to that moving lorry."

Woody flipped a switch on the remote control from forwards to turbo. The toy car roared off.

Lenny, the toy binoculars, was watching the scenery out the back of the lorry when he spotted Woody and Buzz chasing after them. "Guys! Look! There's Woody—and he's got Buzz with him!"

Bo peeped through Lenny's lenses. "It *is* Buzz! Woody was telling the truth!"

"Oh, no!" Slinky moaned. "What have we done?"

"Rocky!" Bo Peep ordered. "The ramp!"

Rocky crawled towards a lever and pulled, releasing a four-foot-wide ramp.

"Hold on to my tail!" Slinky woofed. He crawled down to the end of the ramp and held out his paw.

Woody handed the remote to Buzz and grabbed Slink's hand.

"Hurray!" the toys cheered.

But suddenly the toy car began to slow down and swerve. As the moving truck pulled ahead, Slinky's coiled-spring middle stretched out . . . and out.

"Speed up!" Woody ordered Buzz.

"I can't! The batteries are running out!"

Slinky's spring was stretched as far as it could go. When his paw slipped out of Woody's hand, he snapped back into the truck, scattering the toys like bowling pins.

The toy car coughed and choked, then sputtered to

a stop. Woody and Buzz watched helplessly as the moving lorry drove on without them.

Woody threw down the remote. "Aw, great!"

Buzz sighed, then jumped to his feet and grabbed the sheriff's sleeve. "Woody! The rocket!"

Woody stared at the rocket still taped to Buzz's back. "Buzz! The match!" Woody searched his vest. Smiling, he pulled out the kitchen match Sid had stuck in his pocket. "Yes! Thank you, Sid!"

Woody rushed round to the rocket on Buzz's back and struck the match. He hoped the words *the big one* were not an exaggeration.

Just then a car whizzed over them, and a gust of wind blew out the flame. Woody fell to his knees and pounded the street. "No, no, no, nooooooo!"

Buzz couldn't stand to see a cowboy cry. He leaned forward to pat him on the shoulder, casting a shadow across Woody's face.

But the sunlight streaming through Buzz's helmet acted just like Sid's magnifying glass. A tiny white-hot dot shone down on the back of Woody's hand.

That's it! Woody thought. Quickly he jumped up and aligned the pinpoint of concentrated sunlight with the fuse. He and Buzz watched hopefully.

At last—the fuse caught fire!

"You did it!" Buzz cried. "Next stop—Andy!"

Woody grabbed hold of the car. Buzz grabbed hold of Woody and aimed the rocket straight ahead.

The rocket ignited, blasting Woody and Buzz down the street so fast, the car often flew inches above the tarmac. Woody struggled to hang on.

Soon the moving lorry came into sight. Hamm and Mr Potato Head herded the flustered toys up against the side walls, out of the way.

Seconds later the car slammed into the ramp. But the impact forced Woody to lose his grip. As the car hurtled into the moving lorry, the rocket veered up into the sky.

"Buzz!" Woody shouted. "I think this is the part where we blow up!"

"Not today!" Buzz shouted confidently. He pressed a button on his chest, and his toys wings sprang open—separating him from the rocket.

Woody covered his eyes. But Buzz flew steadily, secure now in the knowledge of who he was and what his true limitations were. So he was a toy; he'd be the best toy he could be. With easy confidence he manipulated his body like a glider, swooping under electricity cables and soaring gracefully towards the moving truck.

But then they flew past it.

"Buzz! We missed the moving lorry!"

"We're not aiming for the moving lorry," Buzz replied.

Buzz tilted a little to the left, spun them in a

graceful loop, then sailed through the open sun roof of the Davis family van.

Buzz and Woody landed in an open box of odds and ends in the back seat—right next to Andy.

At just that moment Andy sighed and turned away from the window. He glanced at the box.

Woody the cowboy sheriff and Buzz Lightyear, space ranger, lay tucked in the box, their faces arranged in the exact same smiles they'd worn the first day Andy laid eyes on them.

"Hey!" Andy squealed. "Wow!"

"What is it?" his mum called over her shoulder from the front seat.

"It's Woody—and Buzz!"

"Great," Mrs Davis said. "Where were they?"

"Here!" Andy cried. "In the car!"

Mrs Davis chuckled and shook her head. "See? What did I tell you? Right where you left them."

Andy hugged both toys as if he would never let them go.

At the next light Mrs Davis took a left turn. Then the van—full of three happy people and two very delighted action figures—drove down the road, towards a new home, towards the future.

Above them, Sid's rocket exploded like fireworks in the evening sky.

EPILOGUE

A few months later, in a place far away . . .

Sunrise sparkled on the new-fallen snow that blanketed the neighbourhood.

Andy's new neighbourhood.

A cheery wreath hung on the front door. Lights twinkled around the frosty picture window, through which an early passerby could see Andy's family gathered around a beautifully decorated Christmas tree.

It looked like a scene on a Christmas card.

Inside the house it was warm and cosy, the air thick with the gentle harmony of Christmas carols and the sweet scent of hot chocolate.

Even this early, Andy was wide awake, poking and prodding the presents beneath the tree. "Which one can I open first?" Andy asked his mum.

Mrs Davis sipped her coffee and smiled sleepily. "Why don't we let Molly open one first?"

Andy knew which one he wanted his sister to open. Grinning, he picked up the present he'd bought just for her. Molly squealed merrily and reached for the shiny package.

Half way up the tree a blinking red Christmas light moved a quarter of an inch. The scented green needles parted slightly. And a small green army man the size of an ornament peeped out, scanning the terrain through his tiny green binoculars. Behind him, soldiers clung to silver tinsel as they climbed into the tree. Another soldier reached for the knob on the baby monitor, wedged between some sturdy branches.

Sarge nodded in satisfaction. Operation Christmas Presents was proceeding according to plan.

Upstairs in Andy's new room the receiving end of the baby monitor on top of the bedside table crackled with static.

"Frankincense—this is Myrrh," Sarge's voice announced. *"Come in, Frankincense."*

Buzz leaned forward from his spot on Andy's bed.

Beside the monitor Hamm called out: "Hey, heads up, everyone! It's showtime!"

Andy's toys—old and new, shiny and worn— chattered excitedly as they gathered on the floor below. The mood was joyous; the fear they'd known on Andy's birthday seemed long forgotten.

Woody was half way to the nightstand when a shepherd's crook yanked him backwards. Bo Peep smiled up at the handsome sheriff.

Woody rubbed his neck. "Listen, Bo, there's gotta be a less painful way to get my attention."

Bo Peep giggled. She pointed up with her crook.

Woody looked up. Bo Peep's sheep hung over the edge of Andy's bed, dangling sprigs of Christmas greenery above the two dolls' heads.

"Say," Woody speculated. "Is that . . . mistletoe?"

Little Bo Peep nodded. "Merry Christmas, Woody!" Then she flung her arms round the sheriff and dipped him backwards for a big old-fashioned movie-star kiss.

"Quiet, everyone," Buzz called out. "Shhh!"

At last the joking and gossiping toys settled down to listen to Sarge's report.

"Molly's first present is . . . Mrs Potato Head! Repeat. A Mrs Potato Head."

Hamm laughed, clapping Mr Potato Head on the back. "Way to go, Idaho!"

"Gee," Mr Potato Head said. "I'd better shave." He whipped off his moustache piece and grinned.

Woody climbed up onto the bed and sat down beside Buzz. The spaceman nodded hello, then stifled a grin and politely didn't mention the lipstick smears all over Woody's face.

"Come in, Frankincense," came Sarge's voice again.

"*Andy is now opening* . . ." Static made his voice difficult to understand.

Buzz leaned closer.

". . . *larger box . . . can't see* . . ." The static seemed to be getting worse, forcing Buzz to bang on the side of the monitor.

"Buzz," Woody said, tipping his cowboy hat back on his head. "You're not worried, are you, pal?"

"No!" Buzz said defensively. "Uh, are you?"

Woody slung his arm round the shoulders of his best friend and chuckled. "Now, Buzz, what could Andy possibly get that is worse than you?"

Downstairs Andy had just unwrapped the answer to that question.

"*A puppy!*"

Our favourite Babysitters are detectives too! Don't miss the new series of Babysitters Club Mysteries:

Available now:

No 1: Stacey and the Missing Ring
When Stacey's accused of stealing a valuable ring from a new family she's been sitting for, she's devastated – Stacey is *not* a thief!

No 2: Beware, Dawn!
Just *who* is the mysterious "Mr X" who's been sending threatening notes to Dawn and phoning her while she's babysitting, *alone*?

No 3: Mallory and the Ghost Cat
Mallory thinks she's solved the mystery of the spooky cat cries coming from the Craine's attic. But Mallory can *still* hear crying. Will Mallory find the *real* ghost of a cat this time?

No 4: Kristy and the Missing Child
When little Jake Kuhn goes missing, Kristy can't stop thinking about it. Kristy makes up her mind. She *must* find Jake Kuhn . . . wherever he is!

No 5: Mary Anne and the Secret in the Attic
Mary Anne is curious about her mother, who died when she was just a baby. Whilst rooting around in her creepy old attic Mary Anne comes across a secret she never knew . . .

No 6: The Mystery at Claudia's House
Just what is going on? Who has been ransacking Claudia's room and borrowing her make-up and clothes? Something strange is happening at Claudia's house and the Babysitters are determined to solve the mystery . . .

No 7: Dawn and the Disappearing Dogs
Dawn decides to try her hand at *pet*sitting for a change, and feels terrible when one of her charges just . . . disappears. But when other dogs in the neighbourhood go missing, the Babysitters know that someone is up to no good . . .

No 8: Jessi and the Jewel Thieves
Jessi is thrilled to be taking a trip to see Quint in New York, and thinks that nothing could be more exciting. But when they overhear a conversation between jewel thieves, she knows that the adventure has only just begun . . .

No 9: Kristy and the Haunted Mansion
Travelling home from a game, Kristy and her all-star baseball team are stranded when a huge storm blows up. The bridges collapse, and the only place they can stay looks – haunted . . .

No 10: Stacey and the Mystery Money
When Stacey gets caught with a fake banknote, the Babysitters are astounded. Can *counterfeiters* really have come to Stoneybrook? The Babysitters have to solve the mystery, clear Stacey's name *and* save their reputation . . .

Look out for:

No 12: Dawn and the Surfer Ghost
No 13: Mary Anne and the Library Mystery
No 14: Stacey and the Mystery at the Mall

The Babysitters Club

Need a babysitter? Then call the Babysitters Club. Kristy Thomas and her friends are all experienced sitters. They can tackle any job from rampaging toddlers to a pandemonium of pets. To find out all about them, read on!

No 37: **Dawn and the Older Boy**
No 38: **Kristy's Mystery Admirer**
No 39: **Poor Mallory!**
No 40: **Claudia and the Middle School Mystery**
No 41: **Mary Anne vs. Logan**
No 42: **Jessi and the Dance School Phantom**
No 43: **Stacey's Emergency**
No 44: **Dawn and the Big Sleepover**
No 45: **Kristy and the Baby Parade**
No 46: **Mary Anne Misses Logan**
No 47: **Mallory on Strike**
No 48: **Jessi's Wish**
No 49: **Claudia and the Genius of Elm Street**
No 50: **Dawn's Big Date**
No 51: **Stacey's Ex-Best Friend**
No 52: **Mary Anne and Too Many Babies**
No 53: **Kristy for President**
No 54: **Mallory and the Dream Horse**
No 55: **Jessi's Gold Medal**
No 56: **Keep Out, Claudia!**
No 57: **Dawn Saves the Planet**
No 58: **Stacey's Choice**
No 59: **Mallory Hates Boys (and Gym)**
No 60: **Mary Anne's Makeover**
No 61: **Jessi and the Awful Secret**
No 62: **Kristy and the Worst Kid Ever**
No 63: **Claudia's ~~Freind~~ Friend**
No 64: **Dawn's Family Feud**
No 65: **Stacey's Big Crush**

Look out for:

No 67: **Dawn's Big Move**
No 68: **Jessi and the Bad Babysitter**
No 69: **Get Well Soon, Mallory!**
No 70: **Stacey and the Cheerleaders**

Babysitters Specials:

Babysitters on Board!
Babysitters' Summer Holiday
Babysitters' Winter Holiday
Babysitters' Island Adventure
California Girls
New York, New York!
Snowbound
Babysitters at Shadow Lake
Starring the Babysitters Club
Sea City, Here We Come!
The Babysitters Remember